PARADISE FOUND

PARADISE FOUND

Dorothy Vernon

This Large Print book is published by BBC Audiobooks Ltd, Bath, England and by Thorndike Press®, Waterville, Maine, USA.

Published in 2006 in the U.K. by arrangement with the Author.

Published in 2006 in the U.S. by arrangement with Juliet Burton Literary Agency.

U.K. Hardcover ISBN 1–4056–3539–8 (Chivers Large Print)
U.K. Softcover ISBN 1–4056–3540–1 (Camden Large Print)
U.S. Softcover ISBN 0–7862–8151–0 (British Favorites)

The text of this Large Print edition is unabridged.
Other aspects of the book may vary from the original edition.

Set in 16 pt. New Times Roman.

Printed in Great Britain on acid-free paper.

British Library Cataloguing in Publication Data available

Library of Congress Cataloging-in-Publication Data

Vernon, Dorothy.
    Paradise found / by Dorothy Vernon.
        p.   cm.
    "Thorndike Press large print British favorites."—T.p. verso.
    ISBN 0–7862–8151–0 (lg. print : sc : alk. paper)
    1. Large type books. I. Title.
PR6072.E737P37 2005
823'.914—dc22   2005023821

CHAPTER ONE

The doorbell rang. Now who could that be? A double rap followed, answering Zoe's question. That was Tony's knock. The frown that came to her face went with neither the engagement ring on her dressing table nor the white wedding gown that hung on the outside of her wardrobe. It did, however, tie up with the fact that she had just stepped out of the shower and her hair was still dripping onto her naked body. It was unlucky for the bride to see the bridegroom on the eve of their wedding, but to her consternation she realized that that superstition wasn't the sole reason for her reluctance to admit Tony. She shrugged away her prudishness. Why bother about Tony seeing her like this? After tomorrow . . .

A second double rap cut off her thoughts. Sighing, she pulled on a short toweling robe, slid her feet into a pair of bedroom mules, and went to answer the door, drying her hair with a towel as she went.

She gasped. 'What are you doing here?' The words would have served for Tony, who was supposed to be on a stag night outing with his friends, but not the belligerent tone. That went better with her follow-up accusation. 'That was a dirty trick to pull, Matt Hunter.'

'Trick? What trick?'

1

'You know.'

'The knock, you mean?'

'What else? You knew that I'd think it was Tony.'

'Did I?' The slow indifference of his tone was at odds with his active gaze, which swept over her scantily clad body and the long shapely length of her legs, not offensively, yet creating a disturbance in the pit of her stomach which brought home to her the fact that she was still susceptible where he was concerned. His gaze lifted, night black and sharp with male interest, locking with her eyes and making it impossible for her to look away. 'You're even more beautiful than I remembered.'

'You're even more audacious than I remembered. I'm getting married tomorrow. Why did you have to turn up now, after all this time? Couldn't you have shown enough consideration to stay away, tonight of all nights?'

'You've got it the wrong way round. It's consideration for you that brings me here. I thought it would be less traumatic for us to meet in the privacy of your apartment than in church.'

She bit her lip. 'You intend to be there, then?'

'That's not very friendly. If you didn't anticipate seeing me again, you shouldn't have got involved with my nephew. Your future

2

mother-in-law happens to be my only sister. No way could I miss Tony's wedding.'

'I didn't know you were that close.'

'We aren't. Perhaps I should have said, no way could I miss your wedding.'

It was like a knife in her heart. It had been her long-ago hope that Matt would be at her wedding, but she had seen him in a more prominent role than that of a guest.

'Why did you have to come, Matt?' she asked anguishedly.

'To bring your wedding gift,' he replied prosaically. 'I thought you might want to wear it tomorrow. The lucky something blue.'

'How very thoughtful of you!'

'Aren't you going to ask me in? You're not very adequately covered. And your hair's wet,' he said, taking the towel from her hand and giving her hair a brisk rub. 'I wouldn't like to have it on my conscience if you caught cold.'

'I'm tougher than I look, and you haven't got a conscience,' she said, snatching the towel back again, but nevertheless holding the door open for him to come in.

'M'm, an improvement on your old place,' he said, glancing round with interest. 'Of course, I always knew you'd get on in the world.'

'As insulting as ever, Mr. Hunter.'

'I didn't mean it as an insult, Miss Fortune. Just stating a fact. Do you think that Tony knows?'

3

'That you and I used to be friends, you mean? Not from me. I saw no point in telling him at the beginning, and then—'

'And then you couldn't tell him because it pointed to deception?' he said, a curious smile that made no sense to her playing about his mouth.

'Yes, that's the way it went.'

'We were rather more than friends, Zoe. Our relationship was much warmer than that implies.'

'You never got me to bed.'

'I could have. I remember once, the last time, the barriers were right down. You were ripe for the taking. I was very, very tempted. But, you were too young and—'

Her fingers itched to slap his smirking face. She flattened the palm of her hand against the rough toweling of her robe and gritted her teeth. 'Say it.'

There had been bitter irony in their names. Fortune and Hunter. Because that's what he had firmly believed she was: a fortune hunter. She had admired his life style—who wouldn't have been impressed by the places he went to, the type of car he drove, that special polish and assurance that wealth gives? He had once asked her if it would have made any difference to the way she felt about him if he'd driven an old heap and only been able to afford to take her to coffee bars, which was all her dates could usually manage. She had been so naive that it had never occurred to her to lie. She had replied truthfully that it would have made a great deal of difference. If he had never amounted to anything, he wouldn't have been the Matt who fascinated her out of her mind. All the same, it wasn't his full wallet that attracted her, but his commanding personality, his rapier wit and his intelligence. She hadn't explained it very well. Or perhaps she had been up against a disproportionate amount of cynicism that would have defeated even the most plausible tongue. People, men as well as women, fawned over him for what he had. He was rarely accepted for himself.

'Actually, you jumped the gun just now,' he said. 'When I asked if Tony knew, I didn't mean about us. I was asking if Tony knew that you were marrying him for his money.'

'His money!' That was ludicrous. Tony believed that money was for spending. It ran through his fingers and would never be allowed to accumulate.

'If you're splitting hairs, I'll rephrase. His prospects, then.'

'In spite of your being his boss, I would have said they were only average.'

'He gets a fair deal. I fulfill my obligation by employing him. In return, he gives me a good day's work for a good day's pay. I see to that. But that's not what I was referring to. You're not telling me that you don't know that Tony is my heir.'

'That's news to me. But anyway, even if I had known, what would that amount to? Let's face it, you're a young man yourself; there's only ten years' difference in your ages. You'll marry and have children of your own, and Tony will be cut out.'

'That could happen, but it's unlikely. I'm thirty-five. I'm too used to my freedom. The acquisition of a legitimate heir isn't a good enough reason for giving it up.' He was standing close, tensely regarding her. It showed in the unsmiling mouth, which was too sensual to be called hard, the frown matting his deeply suntanned features; the thoughts it was safer not to speculate upon in the bright black eyes. His eyes narrowed; that fascinating mouth pursed. 'How long has it been, Zoe? Women are usually better at dates than men.'

Her mouth was unbearably dry. She swallowed to moisten it, and his eyes followed the telltale ripple running along her throat. 'Five years,' she said huskily.

'As long ago as that. You amaze me. And you were . . . ?'

'I was nineteen.'

'You don't look much older now.'

'You've got me at a disadvantage.'

That was nothing new. He always did. But she meant that he was fully dressed and therefore more in command of himself and the situation than she could hope to be. Her contrasting lack of clothes made her feel vulnerable, yet, strangely, she wasn't embarrassed. Things came back: how acutely feminine he had always made her feel; the way he had stroked her senses and accelerated her pulse just by looking at her, an acceleration she was fighting to steady at that very moment.

A droll, 'Oh?' barely parted his lips.

'If you're staying, I should make myself decent.'

'You look all right as you are. Regrettably, I can't stay. I'm joining your fiancé's stag party. Thanks for the invitation, all the same.'

'I wasn't inviting anything. I was just being sociable to my future'—she couldn't resist the jibe—'uncle by marriage,'

His jaw tightened. He hadn't liked that. She knew that she shouldn't be so pleased about it because that meant she was letting him get under her skin again. She must concentrate on her affection for Tony and remember how well they got on together. Tony had chased her with matrimony in mind from the very beginning. He was clean-living and honorable and would make her a good husband. Matt had never once considered asking her to marry him. He didn't intend to get married, ever. He was content to let Tony be his heir; with that need satisfied, he would never be short of a woman to fulfill his physical requirements. Unfortunately, knowing all that wasn't helping her as much as she would have liked.

'I'll hand over your present and go,' he said.

'Something blue, you said?' She was intrigued, despite herself.

'To match your eyes. I never thought about the "wearing something blue" bit tomorrow until Nerissa made that comment. I'd like to put it on for you, if I may?'

'It's not a garter, is it?' she asked suspiciously.

A smile quivered on his mouth. 'I wish it had been now. Unfortunately, no. I didn't think of that. I must be getting slow in my old age.'

'I find that hard to believe.'

He took a flat, oblong box from his breast pocket. 'I thought about a dinner service but decided on something more personal, although not as personal as a garter,' he quipped dryly. He snapped open the box and lifted out a sapphire pendant on a fine gold chain.

'It's beautiful,' she said.

'Turn around,' he instructed.

She did so, lifting her hair to make it easier for him to fasten it round her neck. The brush of his fingers on her skin sent shivers through her system to shame her. She should only be that responsive to Tony's touch. Surprise held her rigid as his lips replaced his fingers on the nape of her neck. She didn't seem capable of throwing off the arms that twisted her round until she was fully facing him any more than she could deny the hot tingling glow that raced through her as his mouth possessed hers.

Her pliant body remembered and yielded to the hands pressing against her back, forcing her to arch into his unyielding male strength, crushing her softness against the potent masculine length of him. Yet the moment she came to her senses she had no difficulty in getting free. She gained her release so quickly that she realized that he had been waiting for some sign, a stiffening away to suggest that his kiss was repugnant to her. She hadn't recoiled quickly enough; come to that, she didn't think she had recoiled from him at all? It had been the hammering of her own conscience that she had backed away from. Her body felt alive in a way it never had before in any man's arms. Not even Matt's, except, perhaps, for one unforgettable occasion. For the most part, his kisses of five years ago, the tempered caresses of his free-roaming hands, had been enough, and he hadn't awakened this aching need in her. Nor was that the only shock she experienced. She looked into his eyes and held her breath at the look of triumph she read there. He had done it on purpose to make her aware of her need, to show her the difference and make her face up to the truth. Tony had never aroused this reaction in her, and, damn him, he knew it!

Dear heaven, how could she view the restraint of a kind and loving fiancé and compare it unfavorably with this animal behavior? And that, she thought, was an insult to the animal kingdom. It had been unforgivable of Matt, especially as she knew that he hadn't acted on irresistible impulse. He had done it deliberately; he had probably plotted the scene in his mind in the jeweller's shop when he bought the pendant. It was his way of punishing her for presuming to marry his nephew.

She had taken a hard fall for Matt, but on his side it had been strictly for laughs, not to be taken seriously. She had amused him for several months and had been dropped with a suddenness that had left her feeling emotionally bruised. Anyway, it had all ended five years ago. She had seen the dangers of encouraging anything serious between her and Tony, but she had thought she was being melodramatic. Despite the lack of family unity—Matt had made no move to introduce her into the circle and rarely spoke of his relatives—she had accepted the fact that she couldn't marry Tony and not expect not to have to rub shoulders with Matt on the odd social occasion. She had anticipated that there might be a slight embarrassment, but nothing of any consequence.

'That was hateful of you, Matt Hunter. How could you do it?'

'It was easy . . . very easy. Like me to show you again?'

'No, just get out.'

10

'I'm not apologizing.'

'I would have been surprised if you had. Such conduct would be much too gentlemanly.'

'I wouldn't be contemptuous of anyone's conduct, if I were you. What I did wasn't so outrageous. I took you in my arms and I kissed you. The sparks that ensued were a mutual effort. I'm not apologizing because it would be a lie to say I'm sorry. When you opened the door to me, wearing not a smudge of makeup and very little else, it came over me how delectable you looked.' His gaze ran the length of her brief toweling robe, sending tingles through the flesh the towel concealed from him. His subsequent inspection of her face encountered cheeks that were slightly pinker than normal and eyes that couldn't quite meet his. An awareness of the thoughts going on behind her tight expression brought a trace of laughter to his tone, 'Kissing you was good. I'm not ashamed to say that I enjoyed it. If you're honest with yourself, you'll admit that you did, too.'

She considered denying it, but to what purpose? 'Yes, I enjoyed it,' she admitted. 'You always did pack a powerful amount of sex appeal.'

'Sometimes too much for you to handle?'

Her nonchalant shrug was at variance with the quickening of her pulse at the turn the conversation had taken. He had never pushed her, never transcended the limits set by her somewhat strict upbringing, but she had known that he wanted more than she was prepared to give and that he was doubtless getting it elsewhere. She had sometimes wondered if that wasn't partly why he had lost interest in her and called it a day. She hadn't wanted it to end, but she couldn't have been other than the way she was, and it wasn't fair to expect him to change his outlook. Vital and vigorous in everything he tackled, presumably with a sex drive to match, he went out and grabbed life instead of waiting for it to come to him; it was natural for him to embrace every aspect of it to the full. She had still been in her teens, while he had left his twenties, and the gap had been too wide to bridge. And, yes, he had been a lot too much for her to handle.

Just as if his thoughts were running a course parallel to hers, his lids dropped lower over his black smoldering pupils. 'I bet I wouldn't be too much for you now.'

'Too bad you'll never know. You've left it too late to find out.'

The atmosphere was electric, had been since he came in, and the moment she opened her mouth it occurred to her that she was going about stopping things the wrong way. She knew that Matt would take her statement as a challenge.

The vibrant look he sent her stopped her breath. 'Don't cheat by marrying Tony.'

12

'I won't cheat on Tony. What just happened was a one-time shot. I'm prepared now. I'm not likely to mistake it for anything other than what it is: a base physical response, which I'm human enough to have found pleasure in. I'll see that it doesn't happen again. So don't worry on Tony's behalf. I'll play fair.'

'Oddly enough, I was thinking of you, not Tony. He's not strong enough for you, Zoe. He's not his own master, so he can never be yours. He's a boy, and always will be. You need a man.'

'I don't want a man to be my master. I want to be his equal.'

'I think balance is a better quality to aim for in a relationship. It's impossible for a man and a woman to be equal in all spheres. In some things the woman should be superior, in others the man. With the right man, you'd balance well,'

'You?' she scoffed. 'Don't pretend any interest in me. You haven't wanted to come near me in the last five years.'

'There were reasons,' he said, reflectively stroking his fingers down a hairline scar that crossed his right eye and ran down to his cheek, so faint as to be barely visible. It hadn't been there when she'd known him.

'You must have been aware of my engagement to Tony. Why wait until now to try to foul things up between us?'

'I knew Tony was getting married—to a

humdinger, according to him. Odd that he never mentioned your name. I didn't know that until I turned up at the house and Nerissa divulged it. Otherwise I would have been round sooner to save you from yourself.'

'What a dog in the manger attitude. You don't want me, at least—'

'Before you added that rider I was on the point of correcting you. I could want you very much. But I'm touching on that base physical thing again—the word "base" being your choice and not mine—which you seem to abhor. I think that when two people make the right kind of chemistry they should appreciate it, not turn their noses up at it.'

'I don't want a purely physical involvement with you, or with any man, for that matter. You wanted more than a light flirtation, and I wasn't interested in a heavy but brief affair. And nothing has altered on that score. I want something solid and lasting, marriage and children, not only a shared bed but a shared life, and that's what I'm going to have with Tony. Nothing, but nothing, is going to come before my marriage. I'm taking this so seriously that I've even given up my receptionist's job at the hotel because of the evening hours involved. When Tony comes home from work, I'm going to be there.'

She hadn't meant to work up to such an impassioned speech, but she was trembling with the forces that had built up in her. She

14

had found deep pleasure in being held and kissed by him, but there was more to life than that.

'Do you love Tony?'

For the life of her she couldn't give a straightforward, honest yes, because Matt's return had confused everything for her. So she parried that one by saying, 'Would I be marrying him tomorrow if I didn't?'

The slant of his mouth was doubting, but he merely said, 'And how about Tony? Does he love you?'

'He says he does, and he's never given me cause to disbelieve him.'

His gaze locked with hers for a heart-stopping moment; then his expression went curiously blank. 'In that case, there's nothing more to be said.' With that he turned on his heel and left.

But Zoe wasn't convinced that he had meant it. She locked the door after him, then wandered back into her bedroom, needing to look at her wedding dress . . . She touched it for reassurance but got none. It was a beautiful dress. Since she didn't have a mother of her own, Tony's mother, Matt's sister Nerissa, had gone with her to help with the choice. Yet she had needed no help. It had been the first one she tried on once she decided to go all out and get a gown, and it was perfect for her in every way. Done in pure ivory, it was classically simple, and while it showed her figure off to its best advantage, it was also demurely right for the occasion.

For a long time she had had the feeling that everything was going too well for her and had been suspicious of it. She experienced no earth tremors when she was with Tony, but she felt a deep and warm affection for him, and when he had asked her to marry him, it had seemed right to say yes.

She could never be sure why she had agreed to go out with him when he first asked her for a date. She had known that he was Matt's nephew, and even if she hadn't had positive knowledge of that fact, there would still have been a certain poignancy in their similar looks. Both were tall, with wide shoulders and deeply muscled chests. Matt had the narrower waist and hips, but he exercised more and didn't indulge to excess in food and drink. If Tony didn't pay more attention to his diet and moderate his drinking, or if some caring woman didn't take him in hand, he would have a paunch by the time he was Matt's age. Zoe firmly believed that when she was his wife her loving influence would take care of that. Tony's hair wasn't as fiercely virile or as dark as Matt's, and his eyes weren't black but more of a dark, spaniel brown, but they were enough alike for it to be self-inflicted pain for Zoe to be with him and look at him.

She had never quite got over Matt, so the question was often in her mind, did she go out with his paler reflection as a next-best substitute, or as punishment for taking too long to recover from her hopeless infatuation? Whatever the reason, very gradually, over the months, Tony's own beguiling personality had infringed itself upon her awareness, and she had begun to accept him, faults and all, for himself, had grown to like him and be very fond of him.

For Tony's sake, Zoe went out of her way to like Tony's mother. Nerissa Talbot hadn't been widowed all that long, and it was natural for a newly bereaved woman to cling to her only son. Zoe made allowances for both of them, guessing that Nerissa had always been overprotective and appreciating that this could account for the streak of weakness in Tony. Nerissa had taken the wind out of Zoe's sails by admitting as much herself while taking pains to point out that she would do her utmost not to be an interfering mother-in-law, and grandmother when the time came, and that it was her dearest wish that she would find a friend in her daughter-in-law. That was fine by Zoe. Kind of comforting. There had still been the stumbling block of Matt, but she'd managed to still any tiny voice of disquiet in that quarter.

It was strange the way Tony never spoke of Matt. After all, Matt was his boss as well as his uncle. On the rare occasion when Matt's name did filter into the conversation, there was a bitterness in Tony's tone that was unattractive. At the risk of being disloyal to her fiancé, she wondered whether Tony's antagonism wasn't based on jealousy.

Matt hadn't inherited a family concern as so many do. He had started with a modest job with a firm of haulers, learning the ropes before graduating to his own haulage business. From small beginnings it had grown into a name to be reckoned with. Although the trading name was just 'Hunter's' now, in the days when Zoe had known Matt it had been 'Hunter & Talbot.' Had the Talbot been a relative of Tony's on his father's side? Was that why Matt had made Tony his heir? And what had happened to the partnership?

The ringing of the telephone broke off her conjectures. When she answered it, Zoe was slightly dismayed to hear Nerissa's voice. At the best of times Tony's mother could hardly be described as a soothing influence. 'Just checking that the bride-to-be is okay.'

'I'm fine, thank you, Mrs. Talbot. It was thoughtful of you to ring.'

'I'm not so old that I can't remember the night before my wedding. I was in a terrible state. You wouldn't believe it.' Oh, yes, Zoe would. Her future mother-in-law twisted her fingers and fidgeted and made a big panic production out of everything. 'I'm pleased to hear you sounding so calm.'

If Nerissa thought that, either she wasn't

very perceptive or Zoe was a better actress than she'd credited herself with being.

'Has my brother been round to introduce himself?'

'Yes, and to bring my wedding gift.'

'Matt is very unorthodox. Anyone else would have waited until morning, but he was most insistent. He's a very forceful man; it's best to go along with him.'

'Yes, I . . . er . . . can imagine.'

'Weddings aren't his scene at all, and he has a very full work schedule. You should be flattered, Zoe dear, that he's squeezed the time in to be here for yours and Tony's wedding. Although why . . . ?'

Was Zoe supposed to say how flattered and thrilled and delighted she was that Matt proposed to attend the next day's ceremony? The words would have stuck in her throat. And what did she make of that puzzling, *Although why?*

Nerissa ended the lengthy pause by asking, 'Did you like the gift he brought you?'

That was easier. 'It's beautiful. I couldn't help but like it.'

'I'm delighted. Matt bought a gift for Tony, too. Cuff links. You can also expect the traditional check.'

'Your brother is very generous.'

'It's easy to be generous when you're loaded,' Nerissa said in a dry, waspish tone that held Zoe's tongue silent. 'Are you glad that you listened to me and decided on the gown?'

Like every girl, Zoe had dreamed of a long wedding gown and a veil, but when the time had come she had wanted to relinquish it in favor of a two-piece suit and less bridallike hat. She had even got her outfit picked out. It would have been different if her parents had still been alive and she'd been getting married from the family home. But they weren't. Zoe had no really close relatives, just distant cousins and one elderly aunt who wasn't in the best of health and couldn't tackle the long journey, so she wouldn't be at the wedding. Another regret was that Tony's maternal grandmother wouldn't be able to come for the same reason. She lived even further afield—in France, the country her husband's work had taken her to in mid-life. She loved the warmth and the people, and on becoming a widow she had seen no reason to pull up stakes and decided to remain in Provence. Zoe had still to meet her.

All in all, anything on a grand scale had seemed pointless to her. But when she hinted at this, Nerissa had practically gone into a state of shock, saying that it wasn't fair to deprive her of the glory of a full-scale wedding. She had looked down her nose, as if there was something improper in Zoe's wish to slide quietly through the big day. And anyway, Nerissa had protested, even if Zoe only had a modest handful of guests she wished to invite, her own large circle of friends would make the numbers up.

'Yes, I'm glad you talked me into it, Mrs. Talbot.'

'I knew you would be. Mothers always know best,' Nerissa came back, not seeming to notice the hollowness of Zoe's tone. 'And now, dear, I'll let you get your beauty sleep. Can't have you looking less than radiant.'

Nerissa rang off then. Sighing, Zoe prepared for bed, knowing full well that she wasn't going to be able to sleep. Tony's dislike of Matt had been obvious all along. Nerissa, while not gushing over her brother, had always been careful to cover up. She had been less attentive just now and had let her true feelings show through. And then there were her own feelings about Matt . . .

Purposefully, she tried to turn her thoughts to other matters, but the effort proved futile. Nerissa had taken most of the wedding arrangements off her hands, including sending out the invitations. At first Zoe had been a little resentful of that. It was her wedding and it seemed as though she wasn't having a hand in it. Tony had pointed out to her that because she didn't have any daughters of her own, it had always been his mother's deep regret that she would never get to arrange a wedding. 'She would have had to stand aside if your mother had been alive, but in the circumstances it's a

21

pity to deprive her, and quite frankly, darling, I think it's a little selfish of you to want to do so,' Tony had recriminated. Zoe had conceded that she supposed it was, and she had given in, if not very happily. It occurred to her now that while an invitation had been sent to Matt, it had been done so merely to observe protocol. A handsome gift had been expected, apparently, but not his presence!

A small, wry smile curved Zoe's mouth. Matt had always been unpredictable. The smile disappeared with her next thought. It had been unpredictable the way he had walked out on her five years earlier.

She had known that he must have been dating other girls at the same time as he was seeing her. He had too much sensuality in his makeup to be satisfied with what he was getting out of their relationship. There was a look about him—she had seen it again that night and remembered it vividly from before— that she had always viewed with wary fascination. A look which said he would have a voracious sexual appetite. So there would have been other women to provide what was lacking in his relationship with her. Perverse creature that she was, even though she hadn't been ready for a full sexual relationship and was glad when he turned off the heat and seemed satisfied with the way things were, she had been jealous of those suspected other women. Yet, in other ways, it had been good. They had got on well together. Occasionally he took an avuncular attitude, but she had thought that was a deliberate cooling process on his part should his thoughts, or desires, get too steamy, and so she had been grateful for it. Most of their time together had been too fantastic for words. Words weren't always needed. They read each other's thoughts so well that sentences often trailed off unfinished. That was why she hadn't been able to believe it, and why it had hit her so hard, when he dropped her without explanation. Even if he didn't want to see her again to tell her that it was over, he could have written, or phoned. He'd had a big cross-Continent haulage job that he said would keep him away for at least a week. He saw her the night before he left, taking her for a meal. He always took her to the best spots, but that night he really outdid himself.

It had been the last thing in elegance. She remembered sitting on a pink velvet Regency chair, and even though queening it was certainly not her style, she had felt rather regal as she sipped vintage champagne and, because she couldn't understand French, watched Matt cope with the menu. She had imbibed just a bit too freely, and she'd felt strangely exhilarated and dangerously reckless.

When he took her in his arms after driving her home she thought about the passionate Continental women he would encounter during the following week. Feminine eyes always followed him with explicit invitation, even when she was with him, so she could use her imagination about what happened when she wasn't there. He could be driving a truck, which he frequently did, because he was the kind of boss who liked to get out on the road and keep close contact with his men, but he would always stand separate from the crowd. All the angry warmth of her thoughts went into her response. She had always had difficulty in keeping herself in check, and it was bliss to let go and shift the onus onto him. He had kissed her in every way imaginable— and in other ways she hadn't imagined. She remembered the musky smell of him, a combination of shaving cologne and the increase of his body heat as her new warmth was discovered and explored. His tongue had traced her mouth, tasting her and testing her responses to kisses of greater depth and intensity. His hands had removed themselves from each side of her face to unbutton the bodice of her dress. She remembered the frustration of all those tiny buttons, so many of them, and then the skin of her breasts tingled as she remembered the gentle but sure touch of his fingers, the sweetness of his lips, the bolder foray of his hands sliding over her hips. He hadn't tried to make love fully to her, . . . but if he had?

It was a question she had asked herself many times since. He had seemed as shaken as

24

she was when he left her, and she had expected him to get in touch with her when he came back. The week passed, then a second, and still no word from him. Eventually the strain was too much. Thinking that something had happened to him—he'd met with an accident, or he was ill—she had phoned his home number but got no reply. So then she phoned his work number. An icy-voiced female had answered; it had been the kind of voice that went with boring tweeds and no-nonsense lace-up shoes, or perhaps Zoe was prejudiced because she didn't like the things the formidable lady said. She had insisted on knowing Zoe's name before giving any information out. And then she had said, very clearly and with cutting explicitness, 'I'm sorry, Miss Fortune, but I am instructed to say that Mr. Hunter is not available.'

Why . . . why? It had made no more sense then than it did now. If Matt didn't want her, why had he come back to torment her? Why hadn't he been decent and stayed out of the picture and let her get married to Tony with a reasonably peaceful mind?

What was she going to do now? Give up Tony, even if she could bring herself to call off the wedding at this late hour? Tony had never been anything but sweet and kind and affectionate toward her. Could she hurt him? As for his mother! . . . She swallowed. In her mind's eye she could see Nerissa throwing up her arms in despair. 'How could you do this to us, Zoe?'

Did she want to give Tony up? Several relationships had started up after Matt had left her high and dry, but until Tony she had never met anyone she would have considered marrying. Irrespective of whether she had accepted Tony for the right or the wrong reasons, it was right for her to get married. She needed someone permanently there, needed a shared future.

Even if she could forgive Matt for the cruel way he had dropped her, she would never be able to trust him again. Matt had always been a loner, self-sufficient and uninterested in settling down with one person. Thinking that he might have changed—that he might have done some soul-searching and decided that he wasn't the solid fortress he imagined, that when it came down to basics he was a flesh and blood man, like every other, who needed someone—was a sure way to heartbreak.

CHAPTER TWO

It was morning. The dawn that crept into her room was as gray as her thoughts. Nothing had been resolved in her mind. It was her wedding day. She glanced across at her wedding dress. It seemed to stare back at her in recrimination, because she still hadn't any idea whether she would put it on or not.

She knew she had to see Tony, tell him everything, and ask him if he still wanted to go through with the wedding. After the way she had deceived him by not admitting that she knew Matt, he might not want to marry her. But if, after hearing her confession, he did, then it seemed to her that the best thing would be to let the marriage take place.

She wasn't fooling herself for one moment that Tony was of the same caliber as Matt. Tony would always need loving understanding and helpful support. But she thought they could make a go of it and enjoy a happy life together. It wouldn't be as idyllically happy as life with Matt could have been. But it was like comparing a modest diamond with a bright, shining star. One was within her reach, the other was not. Would she deny herself a normal life for a dream?

She got up, showered, and dressed. Mrs. Talbot had suggested, tentatively and hopefully, that as she would feel lost on her own in her huge rambling house, perhaps the newlyweds would care to share it with her. For once Zoe hadn't been susceptible to Tony's argument on the value of taking up his mother's kind offer. Kind to whom? She had put her foot down firmly, and now they had an apartment of their own to go to. It did not have an elevator, but the innumerable steps that had to be climbed to reach it and the fact that it lacked the plush comfort of Tony's home didn't matter. What counted was that it would be *their* home.

But until the wedding Tony still lived with his mother. And as she would be there, Zoe chose a sedate, if still becoming, blouse and skirt, instead of the snug-fitting jeans which she wore like a comfortable second skin and which Mrs. Talbot abhorred. Sweet in many ways, she didn't move with the times. Current trends and codes of behavior sent her eyebrows skidding up to her elegant hairline.

Normally, beyond a dab of moisturizer and perhaps a light application of lip gloss, Zoe wouldn't have bothered about makeup for a hurried morning visit, but on inspecting her face and seeing the ravages caused by the turmoil of her thoughts, she decided to use blusher on her pale cheeks and eye shadow to shift the emphasis from the purple crescents beneath her eyes. They were the color of bright sapphires, as Matt had remembered when choosing the pendant for her, so she used a soft, shimmering blue-gray. The incredible length of her lashes needed no enhancing. Luckily they were a darker shade than her hair. Nerissa had wanted her to have her bright russet hair specially styled to take an elaborate headdress, but Zoe had stuck to her decision to leave it as it was, saying that she wouldn't feel like herself and therefore wouldn't be comfortable otherwise, and she had found a simple half-hoop of flowers that complemented its length and simple style. Now she brushed it out until the burning highlights danced like flames; she revelled in its healthy bounce as she checked her appearance all round. Even though the inner turmoil was still there, every brick of the outside was in place—if no one looked too closely at the dark shadows under her eyes.

Nerissa was already up when Zoe arrived, and she answered the door herself. Usually it was the maid who did that chore.

'Zoe!' Nerissa's pale hazel eyes signaled her alarm. 'What is it?'

'It's nothing, honestly. At least, nothing to worry about,' Zoe said as Nerissa widened the door to let her enter. 'I just have to see Tony.'

Nerissa Talbot was a tall woman, claiming three inches more than Zoe's five feet five. Even at that early hour she was immaculately turned out in a trim dress of multicolored checks and presented a fresh morning image. Her fine hair was beautifully coiffed for the wedding, but then, it always had that 'just set' look. Her skin was fairer than either Matt's or Tony's, but she bore them a strong family resemblance, though her features were slightly softened by her femininity. She was considerably older than Matt; Zoe judged her to be in her late forties, possibly even fifty. Not in the whole of their acquaintance had Zoe thought of her as being a hard woman, until that moment.

A hint of color touched Nerissa's cheekbones as she said, 'That's not possible, Zoe.'

'I know you think it's unlucky for us to see one another before we get to church, and I wouldn't offend your principles if it wasn't important. Please, it will only take a moment or two, and then—'

'It isn't that. The fact is'—Nerissa bit her lip and looked troubled, then sighed, realizing the futility of withholding information, although her admission came with extreme reluctance—'you can't see Tony because he isn't here.'

'Not here? Where is he then?'

'I don't know. I wanted to prepare his breakfast myself, it being his last day. I've just taken his tray in. His bed hasn't been slept in.'

'Have you any idea where he can be?'

'Not now that you're here,' came the stilted reply.

'You thought Tony had spent the night with me?' Zoe asked, more amused than offended.

'Yes, I'm broad-minded enough to think that,' Nerissa retorted in the kind of stiff tone that said she really wasn't.

For the first time Zoe saw a flicker of something in her future mother-in-law's eyes that made her realize she might not be quite as much in favor of this marriage as she had led Zoe to believe.

'I suppose Matt and Tony got disgustingly drunk and the pair of them spent the night with another member of the stag party. Men!' Nerissa finished with a shudder.

'Couldn't Matt have taken Tony home with him?' Zoe suggested.

'My brother arranged to stay here overnight. More convenient for getting to the church.'

'Shouldn't you check to see whether he's in his room?'

'I will, but he won't be there. Matt wouldn't have come home without Tony,' Nerissa said with conviction.

On this point Zoe knew differently. Nerissa had her back to the stairs, and as Zoe was facing Nerissa, the man coming down the stairs was visible to her.

'Someone speaking my name in vain? Good morning, Zoe,' Matt said, a vagrant smile touching his mouth, though it didn't wander into his eyes as he studied her appearance.

'Good morning, Matt,' Zoe responded as her heart accelerated, but whether from his prolonged regard of her or hers of him she had no way of knowing.

It seemed possible that he had been in bed when she came in. Perhaps hearing her voice had hurried him down. His hair was still tousled, and a dark shadow covered his unshaven chin. He wore blue denims that were a match for the ones she favored. Their faded color and the way they molded themselves to him indicated long usage and showed off his magnificent physique in a more earthy way than his well-cut suit had. He was still in the process of fastening his shirt. Before he dealt with the buttons and tucked the flapping edge in at the waistband, smoothing it down over his lean hips, the glimpse of a long V-shaped patch of tightly curling black hair made her fingers tingle.

By this time Nerissa had swung round to face her brother. 'Matt! What are you doing here?' As Zoe was now viewing the back of Nerissa's head, the woman's expression was concealed from her, but Nerissa's voice was highly agitated.

'Sister, dear, you kindly asked me to stay. To save me the hassle of crossing town in the mid-morning traffic,' Matt drawled with exasperating slowness, the alertness of his eyes showing that he was summing up the situation.

'I know that,' Nerissa said touchily. 'I meant what are you doing here without Tony?'

'Isn't Tony here?'

'Obviously not! What's the matter with you, Matt? Where did you go last night?'

'Several places. We ended up at the Ace of Clubs. At around twelve-thirty I'd had enough and came home.'

'Leaving Tony there?' Nerissa gasped incredulously.

'Come on, Nerissa. Tony's a grown man. It's

not up to me to tell him when it's time to pack it in.'

A nebulous thought stirred in Zoe's mind. Matt was neither as innocent nor as ignorant as he was making out. 'Was Tony drunk?' she asked.

The black eyes shifted to sweep lazily over her, and his mouth lifted at one corner. 'He looked as if it would take him about a week to sober up. Can't see him being in a fit state to stand up in church this morning.'

She was right in what she thought. Matt had set Tony up, and he was gloating about his triumph. But her hair wasn't the color it was for nothing. 'You did it on purpose!' she screamed, rounding on him in a blaze of anger. 'You deliberately got Tony drunk so that the wedding couldn't take place. How could you do such a vile thing? You won't get away with this, Matt Hunter,' she threatened, almost choking on her own fury.

'Just a minute, Zoe,' Nerissa interceded. 'I don't like having to rebuke you, but I can't stand by and let you talk to my brother in this way. Consider his position. *If* the wedding takes place,' she said with undue emphasis, 'Matt will be your uncle by marriage. In this family we have respect for our elders.'

That was ludicrous. Rather than putting Zoe in her place, it had put Matt in *his*! How Zoe managed not to laugh out loud on witnessing the look on Matt's face she didn't know. In springing to her brother's defense, Nerissa had hit him below the belt.

'Shut up, Nerissa,' he growled. 'I haven't needed you to champion me since I was three years old.'

'Not even then,' Nerissa said soberly. 'You could always look out for yourself.'

'Precisely. It's a lesson men learn at an early age, or they stay boys all their lives and never get to be men.'

'Tony is a man,' Zoe gritted doggedly, remembering back to the day before and the sensual inference he'd injected into telling her that she needed a man.

'In that case, he's well able to take care of himself, and he wouldn't thank me for telling him that he's had enough to drink and it's time for him to come home.'

'Your round,' Zoe said, the glint in her eyes saying that the battle was by no means over.

'No one seems to be showing the slightest concern for my poor son,' Nerissa declared querulously, her former agitation creeping back into her voice. 'What if something has happened to him?'

'I'm sure he'll be all right, Mrs. Talbot,' Zoe comforted. 'He'll be sobering up somewhere. Any moment he'll be phoning to say how sorry he is for causing any distress. Meanwhile, what do I do? Do I stay here and wait or go home and get ready for my wedding, in case Tony does make it in time?' Switching her gaze to glare at Matt, she said, 'Can't you do anything?'

'Presumably you don't mean anything so drastic as substituting for the bridegroom,' he said sardonically.

'Matt, this is no time to joke,' Nerissa chided gently, her worried eyes full of appeal.

Matt shrugged and looked at Zoe in a way that asked, 'Who's joking?' which was just the sort of macabre torment she would have expected from him. 'I suppose I could do some phoning round,' he said. 'Find out if anyone knows where he bedded down for the night.' Several phone calls later he said, 'No joy. No one can recall who Tony left with when the party broke up.'

'Isn't that rather odd?' Zoe asked suspiciously.

Matt snorted. 'You wouldn't think so if you'd seen the condition they were in.'

'Don't you know anyone else to phone?' Nerissa entreated as he walked toward the window.

'Perhaps there is someone,' he admitted, a curious gleam in his eye.

At that moment the phone started to ring.

'There you are,' Zoe gasped. 'That will be Tony now to set our minds at rest.'

No one could have got to the telephone before Nerissa. When she observed the woman's fear-blanched features and quivering fingers, despite her own nervousness, Zoe felt

35

sorry for her. Nerissa's love for her son was as apparent as her anxiety.

Zoe waited with bated breath, willing the tension to lift from Nerissa's face, but instead a stricken moan escaped her lips. 'Oh, God, no!'

Zoe's face mirrored her impatience to know, but even as her mouth opened to form an inquiry, Matt's compelling fingers tightened round her arm. 'If you interrupt it will delay anyone knowing. Nerissa will tell us soon enough.' And so her imagination ran riot as she heard Nerissa say, 'But how is he? . . . You're not? Surely you must know something in spite of that . . . What did you say?' And then eventually, 'That's a mercy, anyway. Yes, I've got the name of the hospital. I'll get there as soon as I can.'

'Don't let whoever it is ring off,' Matt commanded.

'Just a minute, don't—' But it was too late. The phone that Nerissa was holding uselessly in her hand was giving off a dial tone, showing that the connection had been cut. 'She's rung off.'

'She?' Matt asked.

'A girl with a foreign accent. She didn't give her name. She said she wasn't a nurse. Tony fell down a flight of steps. He's broken his leg and cracked two ribs.'

'What kind of accent would you say the girl had?'

36

'I don't know. It didn't have a guttural sound. She could possibly be French. Perhaps she works at the Ace of Clubs and saw the accident. I think I can say almost definitely that she *is* French. The line wasn't as clear as it might have been, but her voice had a very attractive sound to it, not unlike Camille's.' For Zoe's benefit Nerissa explained, 'Camille is a French girl who's working over here. Her grandfather has a house not far from mother's at Les Pins.'

Matt's brow was heavy in conjecture. 'You've never been to the Ace of Clubs.' It was a statement, not a question. 'Have you, Zoe?'

'No. I've heard of it, of course, but I've never been there myself.'

He nodded, then turned back to Nerissa. 'I'll phone the hospital, if you'll tell me which one, and check to see what she says is true.'

'I thought'—Nerissa bit her lip—'Why waste time? Couldn't we just go?'

'No. First we must make certain that it isn't a hoax call, and then there are things to be done.'

'What things?' Nerissa asked.

It was Zoe who supplied the answer. 'A wedding to be canceled. The minister to be told, the caterers, florist, and, of course, the guests. Not to mention the honeymoon booking.'

Zoe thought that Nerissa was going to faint. 'What can we tell everyone? What will they think? The scandal!' she shrieked.

'Who cares?' Matt asked, picking up the telephone directory, ready to thumb through it for the hospital number.

Zoe heard enough of his ensuing conversation to know that it was all true. As he replaced the receiver Matt said, 'A broken leg and two cracked ribs. His condition isn't causing anyone concern but Tony, who won't be feeling too comfortable. He'll only be kept in for a matter of days.'

He might have sounded callous, but Zoe knew that his calm acceptance was to cool Nerissa's hysteria. She seemed to regard having to cancel the wedding as a personal shame. As Matt got on with phoning all the people who had to be informed, Zoe divided her time as best she could between finding the relevant numbers for Matt and trying to soothe a distraught Nerissa, who moaned continuously about all her beautiful arrangements coming to nothing and the degradation of it all.

When they did finally arrive at the hospital it was to find a very sorry for himself Tony, his left leg encased in a cumbersome plaster cast, suffering from an outsize headache, and in pain from his ribs. That he was suffering was obvious from his strained face, which had gone a peculiar shade of gray.

He complained about his rotten luck, and Zoe hadn't the heart to remind him that he himself was responsible for his predicament—with some help from Matt!

It was evening when Matt drove them back to the house.

'What are you going to do, Zoe?' Matt inquired.

'You're welcome to stay here,' Nerissa offered.

Strange as it might have seemed, until that moment Zoe hadn't considered her own plight. She had given up her job and, as of the end of the month, her apartment. Most of her things had already been transferred to the new apartment where, on their return from their honeymoon, they had planned to start their married life.

'Thank you. It's kind of you, but I'll be all right where I am . . . until the end of the month, at least. Perhaps by then? . . .' She shrugged.

Matt said, 'I wasn't looking that far ahead. I was thinking more about now. That's not a bad idea of Nerissa's. Why don't you take her up on it, if only for tonight?'

'I'll be all right. Really.'

'Anyway, surely you'll stay for something to eat?' he persisted.

They had existed all day on snatched sandwiches and cups of coffee, but Zoe said, 'I'm not hungry,' even if that wasn't quite true. 'For goodness sake, stop fussing!'

'Okay. Suit yourself.'

She was doing just that. She'd had a surfeit of Nerissa. If Zoe heard any more of Nerissa's weepings and wailings, she'd go berserk.

They had gone to the hospital in Matt's car. Hers was still outside, where she'd parked it that morning. She automatically assumed that she would drive herself home and toyed idly with the notion of stopping off somewhere for something to eat. She had a hollowness inside her that wasn't altogether due to the traumatic happenings of the day. If she didn't get sustenance soon she would keel over. Because she was fighting a feeling of nausea, she wasn't too aware of what was going on.

'Stay put,' Matt instructed. 'I won't be a second.'

His absence gave Nerissa another opportunity to moan. 'What a dreadful day! My poor boy. What a thing to happen. There's no justice in this life. Some people seem to lead a charmed existence, while others . . .' Her eyes filled with tears.

'Please don't distress yourself, Mrs. Talbot,' Zoe said wearily, feeling that if anyone should be screaming at injustices and kicking up a fuss, it ought to be her.

Matt returned not a moment too soon. Zoe never thought to question the large carrier bag in his hand.

'Ready, Zoe?'

'Yes,' she said, rising from her chair, thinking that he meant to accompany her to

40

the car. 'Goodnight, Mrs. Talbot. Try not to worry too much and get a good night's sleep. Things will look brighter in the morning.' It was trite, but it was the best Zoe could do. She wondered if she ought to kiss Nerissa on the cheek. After all, if things had gone according to plan, the woman would now be her mother-in-law. It looked a very frosty cheek. She managed it, but she thought the kiss was received as unenthusiastically as it was given.

When they reached her car Matt said, 'Keys, please.'

After handing them over, she was surprised when he ushered her round to the passenger seat.

'I don't understand,' she said.

'It's simple. You don't look in a fit state to get home by yourself, so I'm driving you.'

She was too exhausted to argue or to wonder how he would get back. She managed to say, 'I did intend to stop on the way and get something to eat.'

'That's taken care of,' he said, indicating the carrier bag.

And that was how she felt: taken care of. Even though she was still fuming with Matt and held him at least partly responsible for what had happened, it was a nice feeling.

Once inside her apartment, Matt headed straight for the kitchen, where he began to take things from the bag. He'd thought of everything: steak, all the makings of a salad,

41

including dressing, crusty rolls, fruit and cheese, and a bottle of champagne.

'Looks like a celebration,' she said wryly.

'Perhaps it is. Perhaps we're celebrating your not getting married.'

Her chin lifted. 'It's only a postponement. Nothing's altered.'

'If you say so.' Although his lips lay close together in a straight line, there was a blandness about his expression that hinted at inner laughter.

He was still wearing the jeans he'd put on that morning. The thrust of his hips, the arrogance of his stance, was powerfully potent. His shirt was fastened, but she remembered the masculine virility of that coarse curl of hair, and her fingers tingled again, wanting to— She slammed the door shut on that thought and hastily averted her eyes.

His earthy male sexuality attacked her senses. Though he hadn't put a hand on her, it was as if his fingers had curved around her throat. Breathing was difficult, and the resultant lack of oxygen in her lungs made her head swim. She knew that she had to get away from him for a moment to regain control of herself. In spite of the way her body was reacting to his nearness, she wasn't an empty-headed teenager anymore. She had been affected by his sensual magnetism once, had not put up a struggle against it, and in consequence had suffered the heartache of rejection. She had played this scene once and knew the score. To let him get close to her again was to invite a second dose of the pain.

But as her eyes came up again the words of excuse that she had been about to speak were half-strangled by the disturbing scrutiny of his gaze, which was centered on her lips. She had to fight him. Disregarding the aching tightness in her throat, she said, 'I feel grimy. Do you mind if I freshen up before I start on the meal?'

'Take your time. I intended to act as chef anyway.'

In her bedroom the world became a less rocky place, although she did have one bad moment when she saw her wedding gown, all ready to slip on, hanging on the outside of her wardrobe. She thought about bundling it back into its box but decided, that perhaps she needed it there as a reminder. Not the most strong-willed attitude, but still, she had never pretended to be heavy on resolution where Matt was concerned. Hoping that he would be different, that this time he wouldn't kiss and run, was on a par with wishing on the wind.

What foolish segment of her heart had been harboring that thought? The wind was changeable; Matt was not. And something else: If she were stupid enough to let there be a 'this time', it wouldn't stop at kissing. He had walked away from a girl and come back to a woman.

She stripped off her clothes, deciding to go whole hog and take a shower, hoping it would cool her senses. The tiny bathroom communicated with her bedroom, and she didn't bother to lock the door. Matt was too subtle to burst in on her. The cold water felt good on her skin. She emerged, shivering slightly, and gave herself a brisk rubdown, wrapping another towel round her, sarong-style, while she decided what to wear. The choice was limited because so many of her clothes had already gone to the new apartment and she didn't feel like dipping into her honeymoon suitcase. She could still put her hands on two favorite outfits, both influenced by Eastern culture. A Westernized version of the Japanese kimono and a silk pants and blousesuit in an Oriental peacock print. She selected the latter, thinking that she might be a little too accessible in the kimono, which was held in place only by a wide scarlet sash. Sometimes she cinched in the waist of the pants set with a wide belt, but this time she left the blouse to swing loose, letting its volume conceal her figure. In keeping with the Oriental look, she twisted the heavy length of her hair at the nape of her neck, securing it with pins in a figure-eight knot.

The aroma of steaks sizzling under the broiler met her nose when she went to join him. 'M'mmm, that smells good.'

He took a couple of paces forward. 'So do

44

you. You don't look bad, either.'

Sidestepping that remark, and him, she worked her way round to the other side of the table. 'I see you found everything all right,' indicating the place mats and cutlery.

'Glasses defeated me.'

'Ah, problem there. You won't find any. I'm afraid every glass I possess is packed and at the new apartment.

'It'll have to be mugs then,' he said, unhooking two and then deftly twisting the champagne bottle to remove the cork.

'It's sacrilege to drink champagne out of mugs,' she protested, yet she raised hers to her lips the moment it was filled.

'Verdict?' he inquired.

'It's gorgeous.' She had envisioned drinking champagne that night, but not with Matt.

'I wouldn't drink too much until you've got some food in you,' he cautioned. 'Your head will start floating away.'

She met the teasing laughter in his eyes and wondered if he knew that it already was—and taking her ability to think rationally with it. All the good that had been achieved by the short absence from his side was undermined the moment she came within his sphere again.

She occupied herself with tossing the salad while he transferred the steaks from the broiler pan to the plates.

He waited for her to sit down in old-fashioned deference to her femininity. He had always had a way of making a woman feel special. She tried to subdue that lifted-to-the-stars feeling. The higher you went, the greater the fall. Regardless, it was good to sit across a table from him again.

She told herself that she felt better when she'd eaten, more able to cope. They washed the dishes companionably, side by side, while waiting for the coffee to percolate. He'd drink his coffee and go. In a little while the ordeal would be over. She was reluctant to say that it had been easier than she had anticipated, but it was true. He hadn't offered to touch her, but she wouldn't feel out of the woods until he was on the other side of her door.

'Where would you have been now, Zoe, but for events?'

'Portugal,' she said.

'Poor Tony. I don't consider a hospital bed a fair swap for a matrimonial bed. And poor little you, contemplating spending the night alone, on what should have been your wedding night, the first night, as it used to be delicately called. Rather an obsolete expression in these days of anticipating marriage. Perhaps you did the same and so your disappointment won't be as keen.'

'Perhaps.' She wouldn't give him the satisfaction of knowing otherwise. 'Anticipating marriage—that too has a deliciously, old-fashioned flavor to it in these days of sexual freedom. It's late,' she said, springing to her

46

feet. 'I think you should go.'

'If that's what you want,' he said, setting down his coffee cup and lazily standing up.

He stood facing her but made no offer to go, just looked into her eyes for a long tormenting moment. She knew he was going to kiss her, she wasn't going to be let off without that; and to her horror it came to her that she didn't want to be.

'I never before realized how very sensuous a woman could look entirely covered up to the neck. It's much more seductive than a neckline slashed to the waist, the kind that leaves little to the man's own imagination.'

'Cut the talk, Matt.'

'You prefer the action?'

'No, that's not what I meant. Stop it, Matt.'

'Stop what? I'm not doing anything.'

'You do more when you're not doing anything than any man I know.'

'Don't you like the way I look at you?'

'No, I don't.' Neither did she like the husky pitch of his voice; it grated on her senses. Nor the way she wondered if his sons would inherit his dark good looks and proud way of standing with his shoulders back, hips tilted slightly forward and powerful legs splayed at an angle, wondered with a tiny ache low in her stomach that increased as she remembered that the obligatory wife to provide legitimate sons was not in Matt's plan.

She pressed her lips tightly together,

catching the fullness of her lower lip in her teeth. She did it to ease the dryness; she saw his eyes narrow on the movement but only wondered if he found it provocative when she saw him lift his arm and drag the back of his hand across his own mouth.

Instead of replacing the hand by his side, he let his fingers curl round her neck to draw her gently forward, and although the intolerable wait was over, the teasing had only just begun.

His parted lips moved over her forehead, glancing down her temple and following the outer curve of her cheek. Her lips moved compulsively to meet that kiss, but he defeated them by dropping his own lower to brush across her throat in a series of butterfly caresses that left her insensible. She twisted uselessly to nullify the intensity of what she was feeling. When she felt that she couldn't take it a moment longer the teasing stopped and his mouth clamped over hers. It was like a promise fulfilled, and she reveled in it. Her whole being was centered on the joy of that kiss, and his strategy went unnoticed. Her mind was closed to everything but the sensation of his lips on hers, and so she was barely aware of the hand creeping under the looseness of her blouse to close over her breast. It seemed to swell at his touch, its thrusting tip delighting at the abrasion of his thumb. She knew she should push him away, but she couldn't. Nothing else mattered but this ecstasy. His free hand roved over her back, tingling her shoulders and her spine, exciting her hips and bringing her so deliriously close to him that her physical need was almost too acute to bear.

'You don't have to be alone tonight. You don't have to be deprived.'

His voice was barely audible through the mists of her desire. Mists of insanity, more like it. She slumped in his arms, all that intensity of feeling shriveling into a tight knot in her throat.

'No, Matt.' Could that cold voice possibly belong to her?

'No?'

'There's something you seem to have forgotten. I'm wearing another man's ring.'

'I'm not the only one who forgot that.'

'That's true, and I'm ashamed.'

'You don't have to be, Zoe.'

'Don't have to be?' she gasped incredulously. 'Don't try to explain that, Matt. I don't think you could.'

'If that's so, it's not for the reasons you think.'

She didn't believe that. Nothing could justify her behavior. He knew she was right; he had just said that to save face. She was furious with him for his part in what had happened and even more furious with herself for letting herself feel that way about him, for enjoying his caresses. Some of that fury turned back on him. Her driving need was to punish.

She laughed. Even to her own ears it sounded unnaturally high and brittle. 'I'm so sorry, Matt.'

'Sorry?' he queried, frowning.

'Tony being in hospital is only part of my guilt. I feel ashamed for using you. You hit the nail on the head a bit too accurately. Tonight should have been my wedding night, and I felt angry at having to spend it on my own. A woman dreams about that, even if it isn't a new experience.' She couldn't resist that. Then, on a softer, extra hurtful note, 'Perhaps *because* it isn't a new experience. So you see, when you started messing around, I thought, why should I be deprived? But it wouldn't be fair to use you because the man I really want isn't available.'

He didn't say a word. He looked as if he didn't trust himself to open his mouth. His anger was like a black volcano ready to erupt. He turned on his heel and left.

It didn't occur to her to wonder how he would get home, but the knowledge came to her anyway when she heard the urgent revving up of an engine. Of course, he'd taken her car.

It was a long time before she managed to drag herself into her bedroom and, ultimately, to bed. The pressures left from the day were unbelievable. Her wedding hadn't taken place. Her bridegroom lay in a hospital. And what should have been her wedding night had almost been consummated by another man.

CHAPTER THREE

Matt arrived in her car the next day in time for the afternoon visit to the hospital. The pattern of the previous day was followed. Matt, who drove, parked her car where she had parked it the day before. Nerissa was waiting in the house for them, and Matt drove them to the hospital in his car. If Nerissa noticed the below-zero coldness between Zoe and Matt, she tactfully refrained from making any comment.

Tony was obviously still in considerable pain, despite the influence of painkillers, and Zoe, who was not a very demonstrative type of person in public, surprised even herself by holding his hand in an extra loving way and kissing him with the kind of warmth better saved for private moments. She couldn't make up her mind who disapproved most, Matt or Nerissa.

On the way back they talked between themselves, leaving her feeling curiously isolated. When they arrived at the house Nerissa said, 'Are you coming in, Zoe?' Zoe was on the point of saying no. Perhaps that was obvious from her expression, because then Nerissa said, 'I think you should. Practicalities will have to be discussed. In any case, there seems little point in your making the journey to your apartment and then coming back here in time to make the evening visit to the hospital. You may as well stay and have tea with us.'

It seemed a rather grudging invitation, but Zoe concurred. Though how practicalities could be discussed without Tony there was a puzzle to her.

Zoe half expected Matt to decline afternoon tea, but he accepted a cup and she was conscious of his eyes on her when he sat down at the other end of the sofa.

Nerissa settled into her favorite chair on the other side of the long occasional table. 'Now, about the arrangements,' she said, opening the discussion.

'If it's about when a new wedding date can be set, I feel that it's something which Tony and I should decide on our own,' Zoe said firmly.

'A new wedding date?' Nerissa queried.

'We can be married just as soon as Tony is discharged from the hospital, I don't see the point in waiting.'

'My dear, you're surely not expecting Tony to hobble down the aisle on crutches?' Nerissa asked, looking scandalized at the idea.

'Why not? It's been done before.'

'And after subjecting him to that indignity, then what? You'd go back to your new apartment?' Nerissa inquired with the sweetness of someone who had the upper hand.

'Ah!' Zoe said, seeing the, flaw in her own reasoning. 'Tony couldn't manage all the steps. It would be difficult to get him up them, and once there he would be a prisoner.'

'Precisely. It isn't a lot more convenient for him to come back here. We could have a bedroom fitted for him downstairs, but there's the problem of the bathroom, which is upstairs. Luckily, Matt has come up with the ideal solution.'

Zoe was suspicions of anything Matt put forward, but she held her tongue.

'As you know, our mother lives in the South of France. Her house is a split-level and has a ground floor which has bedroom facilities. It will be just perfect for Tony, and his grandmother will be delighted with the arrangement. She's always complaining that she doesn't see enough of the family.'

'You're whisking Tony off to France?' Zoe asked, turning to Matt.

'He'll be in a cast for at least six weeks after his discharge. He's out of commission as far as work is concerned. He can't drive in his present condition, which wouldn't be a problem, because chauffeur service could be arranged for him, but, as everywhere else, there are too many steps for him to cope with at the works. As Nerissa has already told you, mother's house in France has ground-floor bedrooms. But of course, if you can come up with something better . . . ?'

'You know I can't,' Zoe admitted, not liking the way Tony was being removed beyond her sphere. If she didn't care for that, the next bombshell Matt delivered was even less acceptable.

'That's all right, then,' he said. 'The only thing is, I won't be whisking Tony off to France.'

'No?'

'No. You will.'

'Me?'

'We feel that someone should accompany him. Nerissa is tied up with her various committees and charity work. I have a company to run. Also, it will give mother a chance to get to know you. From your point of view there are no difficulties. You've given up your job and your apartment. And perhaps it will make it up to you for missing your honeymoon in Portugal.'

Oh, so that was to be the way of it. Putting on a big smile, she said, 'I think that's a wonderful idea. I'm all for it. I haven't even got round to unpacking my honeymoon suitcase yet, so I'm all set to go.'

It wasn't what she had thought at all, just the opposite! Matt was removing her from *his* sphere. She ought to have been relieved that she wouldn't be in daily risk of encountering

Matt; instead it was as if her legs had been kicked out from under her. She felt an intense need to punish both herself and Matt, herself for her own perfidy and Matt for the brutal way he had flung the news at her. So she stuck her chin out at him and said, 'Only what's to stop the marriage taking place before we go?'

It was Nerissa who answered. 'I should think your consideration for my son would prevent your suggesting such a thing. In Tony's condition, with his ribs the way they are and his leg broken, it would be too much of a strain. Not to mention the big disappointment it would be to me. I want this wedding to be perfect, and it wouldn't be with Tony on crutches.' She paused. Zoe switched from viewing the smirk on Matt's face in time to see the speculative look that touched Nerissa's features. 'I hope this isn't too indelicate a question, Zoe, but it's something I must ask. You seem to be in an inordinate rush about things. Is there any desperate need for you to get married quickly?'

Now who wasn't showing consideration? The woman could have asked when they were alone. 'No,' she said as a hot flood of color stung her cheeks.

*   *   *

The preparations had been masterminded by Matt, so everything was going predictably

55

smoothly. A wheelchair had been at their disposal at the airport to transport Tony through the formalities and onto the plane. Another wheelchair would be there when they touched down to take Tony to the car that would be waiting for them.

'You don't look too happy, darling,' Tony said, taking her hand and looking ruefully at the lone ring on her finger. 'Disappointed that it isn't our honeymoon?'

It wasn't disappointment that had wiped the smile off Zoe's face but fury at Matt's whispered aside on parting. 'Keep Tony's delicate condition in mind, and don't do anything that might put a strain on it.' She wasn't going to tell Tony that, so she sidestepped by counter questioning, 'Aren't you?'

He gave her hand an extra squeeze. 'You know I am; I'm as disappointed as hell. What a silly thing to do,' he said, looking grimly at the ungainly plaster cast stuck out in front of him. The air authorities had been marvelous, ensuring a seat with extra room and providing a leg rest.

'Cheer up, Tony. I'm sure you didn't get drunk deliberately.'

'I didn't even know I was getting drunk. You know how it is. Everyone wanted to buy me a celebration drink, and it would have seemed churlish to refuse.'

'And you certainly didn't fall down the steps

at the Ace of Clubs on purpose,' Zoe said laconically.

It was odd to see Tony's self-assurance slip as he stammered, 'No . . . I . er . . . no, I didn't.'

He was behaving like a small abashed boy. Which was reasonable, she supposed. He undoubtedly felt like an absolute fool for spoiling everything by such a stupid act, and her own fingers, still within his, strengthened their clasp. The look that came to his eyes was a cross between gratitude and wonder.

'I must say, you've been fantastic about this. Most women would have ranted and raved and never let up. And you haven't said one word of condemnation.'

'What would be the point? Anyway, I think you've paid dearly enough in physical discomfort.' She knew that he was in a lot of pain still. She would have known by the look on his face, even if his constant moanings hadn't reminded her of the fact. Men were poor invalids.

'I've really been through the mill,' he grumbled. 'But it's right what they say, no matter how bad a thing seems to be, some good invariably comes out of it. It's made me realize what a treasure I have in you. Not that I didn't appreciate you before, but this has made me see how truly wonderful you are. I'm a lucky man, Zoe.'

The smile she gave him was warm. Away from Matt, beyond the reach of his magnetism, she found she was rediscovering why she had first been attracted to Tony and why she had said she would marry him. His personality wasn't necessarily weaker than Matt's—although, come to think of it, everybody's personality was weaker than Matt's—Tony had come out of a softer mold. After a surfeit of Matt's granite strength there was something very appealing about Tony's human vulnerability.

She was more than a little perturbed, though, at the way Tony was ordering freely from the drinks trolley. She hated to sound as if she were nagging, but she wondered if he was being quite wise.

'Don't forget you're on medication, Tony. The painkillers and what-have-you that the hospital prescribed might not mix with spirits. And anyway, I read somewhere that alcohol is more potent when you're airborne.'

'Great little reader, aren't you? If you were in as much pain as I am, you'd want something to dull the edge.'

She sighed. Who could argue with that? 'Yes, I suppose you're right.'

*   *   *

Just as Matt had promised, a chauffeur-driven car was waiting at the airport to take them to Les Pins, where his mother lived. Zoe was tired after their flight, but her exhaustion dropped away on the fascinating drive. Her eager eyes darted everywhere, much to Tony's amusement. As she pointed out, he had been there many times before, but it was all new to her. She had never even been to France, much less the South of France, which had always had a special charisma.

Although the fashionable resorts of Nice and Cannes were near to hand, Les Pins was not one of the luxury Riviera resorts. It didn't have a casino or a nightclub; there wasn't one millionaire's yacht anchored in the bay. It was a charming old town set against a backdrop of vineyards and fragrant pine woods, with a promenade flanked by acacia, eucalyptus, palms, mimosa, and sidewalk cafés. Zoe fell in love with it at first sight and knew why Matt's mother had chosen to forfeit the country of her birth and settle here.

The houses rose in tiers. The one the driver stopped in front of was, as Matt had said, a split-level and had a quaint charm all of its own, with steps at odd angles and an outside staircase curving to the upper level. But the ground story had no steps; it was completely flat all the way back to the small sheltered garden, which Zoe spied through an arch.

The house was called Les Charmettes. As a tall, keen-eyed, very straight-backed lady came forward to greet them, Zoe knew that she was going to be as truly charmed by the owner as she was by the house.

If they had met in the street, she felt that she would have known this lady to be Matt's mother, even though they didn't share the same coloring. Her hair was white, but a silvery white that suggested she had been fair, and despite living in a sunny climate, she had retained her girlish English rose complexion. The similarity had something to do with the forthright way she looked at Zoe. It wasn't until the assessment was complete that her chin gave a complacent nod and a smile curved her mouth. 'Yes, you'll do. And just as beautiful as Matt said you were when he phoned to make the arrangements.'

Zoe didn't know whether the wild blush stinging her cheeks was because of the close scrutiny she had been subjected to or because Matt had said she was beautiful.

'It was kind of you to say you'd have me, Mrs. Hunter.'

Her hand was taken in a very English handshake, yet she was kissed on both cheeks in the French way.

'It will be my pleasure. I don't get out as much as I used to, and I will appreciate some feminine company and chatter. We must start out as we mean to go on. Mrs. Hunter sounds much too formal. Tony always calls me Nan. I have a rather attractive first name, at least I've always thought so. It's Hannah. I suggest that's what you call me. Hannah means "full of grace and prayer." After four boys, my mother could have used some grace in a girl, and after four boys I was the answer to a prayer.'

'I think it's a charming name, and you have a charming reason for wanting to be called by it. I'd love to call you Hannah, if you're sure it's all right?'

'Zoe, when you come to know me better, you'll find out that I never say anything I don't mean.'

The chauffeur had meanwhile helped Tony out of the car and was equipping him with his crutches. He wasn't used to them yet, and his hobble as he came forward to greet his grandmother was clownish and inept.

"Now who's been a silly boy?' Hannah asked, reaching up to kiss him on both cheeks in the manner she had kissed Zoe.

'Hello, Nan. Looking as young and as beautiful as ever, I see.'

'And I see that you're as full of soft soap as ever. Leave the luggage.' This to Zoe, whose hand had gone down to pick up one of the suitcases. 'That will be dealt with. Come into the house. I thought you'd like a cup of tea first before I showed you where I've put you. Yes, I may live in France and adapted well to the French customs, but I'm an Englishwoman at heart. I drink coffee along with the French, but I still like my cup of tea. I have it specially imported. Matt sees to that for me. Of course, it never tastes quite the same as it does at home. It's the different water, you know. By

61

the way, as you may have discovered already, I talk a lot,' she finished with a small, impish laugh.

'I suppose you find it nice to talk to someone in English,' Zoe commented.

'I just find it nice to talk. I don't miss my native tongue as much as you might think. There's a rather tight English community hereabouts, although I do naturally have French friends, also. Do you speak French, Zoe?'

'Sorry, no.'

'Perhaps you'll pick it up while you're here. Tony never has, but he's lazy. Matt speaks it like a native. Have you ever been to this part of France before?'

'I've never been to any part of France before.'

'Really? There's something especially lovely in seeing a country for the first time. If I didn't love living here so much, I could almost envy you the experience. Pity that Matt isn't here. He could have taken you around,' Hannah said, slotting her arm companionably through Zoe's as she guided her inside, leaving Tony to clomp behind them. 'Long John Silver here isn't going to be much use. And I'm afraid I've tended to make friends of my own age group, so, their visitors excepted, it's no good looking in that direction. And I'm not up to it myself.' This conversation was picked up again over the teacups. The tea trolley, looking very homey with its dainty settings of cakes and scones, was brought in by a very attractive French girl with dark doe eyes who admitted to being able to speak 'a leetle English.'

'Still, you never know, he might pop up unexpectedly, as he usually does,' Hannah said, seemingly out of the blue.

Zoe hadn't followed the drift of Hannah's mind and had to ask, 'Who might?'

'Matt. He rarely rings or writes in advance, just blows in on the wind. Sometimes when the will takes him, other times on a job. Anything that will bring him anywhere within remote shooting distance, he tackles himself, which is nice for me. He's always been a very thoughtful son and a perfect joy to me, once I got over the shock of being a mother again after a gap of fifteen years. Tony's mother, Nerissa, was the obligatory child everyone seems to have at the beginning of their marriage, to prove that they can, I suppose. Matt was my love child. Not that he wasn't fathered by my husband, you understand, but he was conceived in love. It would be nice for you if Matt did suddenly show up to take you places. No matter what your taste is—sailing, sun worshipping, nightclubbing—this coast caters to it. You don't have too far to travel to find a wealth of medieval buildings. And it would be a pity not to cross the frontier and have a mild flutter at the tables in Monte Carlo. Mostly it's not a question of where to go, it's what to leave out. So I'm going to keep my fingers crossed for you and hope that Matt does decide to pay one of his impromptu visits. If you'll excuse me, I'll alert Yvette that we need more hot water.'

'If you point me in the right direction, I'll go,' Zoe volunteered.

'Will you, dear? That's very kind of you. In case Monique isn't about, you'd better take the hot water jug. Yvette is a charming girl, but she does sometimes get carried away, and her "leetle English" may not be up to it. I should explain that Monique is my treasure of a cook and housekeeper.'

'Treasure!' Tony snorted contemptuously. 'She and Pierre ought to have been pensioned off long ago.'

'Lower your voice, Tony,' Hannah reproved sharply. 'You'll get old yourself one day, if you live long enough.' Her tone softened as she turned to speak to Zoe. 'Pierre is Monique's husband. He keeps the garden tidy and does odd jobs about the place. It's true that they're both past the age of retiring. And yes, perhaps they're not as quick as they used to be, but they are fiercely loyal to me. They've been with me for a long time. This is their home. I ask myself, where else would they go?'

Zoe felt that his grandmother had been right in rebuking Tony. As she went for the hot water, she wondered if Matt would decide to turn up. She would have offered to run the errand in any case to save Hannah's legs, but in truth she was glad of the excuse to escape for a few moments to cool her thoughts. Part of her hoped that Matt would come; the saner side of her viewed the possibility with dread.

After second cups of tea, or a third cup, in Hannah's case, Hannah showed them their rooms. Tony's was at the end of the ground floor, next to where Hannah herself slept.

As they left Tony there Hannah quipped, 'You're on my team now, Tony.' Then she explained for Zoe's benefit. 'I'm fantastic for my age, so I'm not complaining. I reckon that I'll see a few of the young ones off yet, but the old gray mare ain't what she used to be. I'm all right on the flat, but my knees creak on stairs.'

Despite her humor, it was no joke, and Zoe felt guilty at dragging her up the stairs to be shown her quarters. She told Hannah that it wasn't necessary and that she would be happy to let Yvette take her up. But Hannah was insistent that she not shirk her job as a hostess. Despite her easy friendship and casual manner in things like forms of address, she took her hostessing duties seriously. But Zoe didn't realize just how seriously until she saw the thought that had gone into the preparation of her *en suite* accommodation. The towels in the bathroom were soft apricot and pink, the soap and toiletries delicately perfumed for feminine use. In the bedroom there was a wide selection of reading matter that included both books and magazines in English. The most thoughtful touch of all was the tea and coffee making facilities, a tin of assorted biscuits, and a tiny refrigerator containing iced drinks and also the requirements for making a light snack.

'You're welcome to make free use of the kitchen at any time of day or night, but I've found out from experience that guests don't always like to. While I'm about it, I don't want you to feel like a guest. You're almost family, and would have been if that idiot of a grandson of mine hadn't come a cropper. Did you blow your top?'

'There wasn't much point.'

'Really? With your color hair I wouldn't have thought you'd be able to help it, unless . . .'

'What?'

'Oh, nothing. Sometimes these old eyes of mine are a bit too shrewd for my own liking. Anyway, I'm glad that you're here. This is one misfortune, Miss Fortune, that has been in my favor. Sorry about the pun, I couldn't resist it.'

Zoe laughed along with her. 'Not many people can. I've got used to it. The favorite one is about my face being my fortune. For obvious reasons, the one I dislike is fortune hunter.'

Hannah nodded. 'You can't be called much of a fortune hunter in nailing Tony. Now if it were Matt! Even the combination of your names—Fortune and Hunter—points to it. I wonder what would have happened if Matt

66

had seen you first,' she speculated.

He did and nothing happened, Zoe thought as she felt the color rising under her skin. She would have been open with Hannah, because Hannah was the sort of person who invited the truth, but for the fact that she still hadn't got round to telling Tony that she had once been friendly with his uncle. If only she'd told him at the beginning. It was the kind of confession that, the longer you put it off, the more difficult it got.

'Zoe,' Hannah was saying. 'Now that's a pretty name. It's the equivalent of Eve, which is the Greek word for life. You'll certainly add a bit of life to Les Charmettes.'

Zoe didn't miss the wry intonation. Hannah was quick. She knew she would have to be careful not to arouse the woman's suspicions, that is, if they weren't already aroused. 'Thank you, Hannah.'

'I wasn't being gracious. I meant it. As you see, Pierre has brought up your baggage. Do you want any help in unpacking? I could send Monique up, or better still, Yvette, who is nearer your age.'

'Thanks, but no. I prefer to do it myself. I feel quite spoiled enough as it is with all this.' She waved her arms expansively.

'I'm glad you like it.'

'I couldn't help but like it.'

'That's nice. I'll leave you to it, then. Come down when you're ready.'

With that Hannah went. What a delightful person Matt's mother was. The thought brought a gentle sigh to Zoe's lips. It was relevant, and more than a little disturbing, that she thought of Hannah as Matt's mother and not her fiancé's grandmother.

There was an easy atmosphere at Les Charmettes, and Zoe fitted in as if she had always belonged. Hannah's select circle of friends made Zoe feel very welcome, and they liked her as much for herself as because she provided the diversion of a fresh face. Especially one so 'young and pretty', to quote André Dupont, a widower who seemed to be one of Hannah's most frequent visitors and who was the grandfather of the Camille whom Nerissa had mentioned. André Dupont asked Zoe if she had met Camille and looked slightly surprised when she said no. 'With any luck, Camille will pay me a visit while you are still here. If not, you must get Tony to introduce you two when you return to England.'

'I will most certainly do that, monsieur,' Zoe had promised.

André Dupont was perhaps a couple of years older than Hannah. Had they been slightly younger, would a romance have blossomed between them? Zoe wondered.

When she mentioned as much to Tony, he looked dubious, but he didn't dismiss the notion out of hand. 'They've always been friends, even when grandfather and Monsieur

Dupont's wife were alive. I would have thought they were too devoted to the memory of their respective partners to consider remarrying, but you never know.'

'What's Camille like?' Zoe inquired.

Tony sent her a sharp look. 'What do you know about Camille?'

'Only that she's Monsieur Dupont's granddaughter. He was telling me that she lived in England, and he thought you might have introduced us.'

'Oh, I see.'

'So tell me what she's like.'

'Charming enough, I suppose,' he said, shrugging to convey indifference.

'Attractive?' Zoe inquired.

'M'mm. You could say she's attractive. Not jealous; are you, darling?'

'Have I cause to be?'

'No.'

'Then why that look?'

'What look?'

'I don't quite know. Sheepish, I think.'

'You're being too fanciful,' he declared loftily. 'Matt's the one Camille has her eye on.'

Zoe wished she hadn't pursued that one quite so relentlessly.

*   *   *

The days passed, perfect days of blue skies and golden sunshine, and Zoe was no more

69

resolved about her feelings than she had been the day she came to Les Charmettes. The deep affection she felt for Tony must surely be love? He didn't make her pulse pound as Matt had, but that wasn't love, that was animal passion. Someone ought to have thrown a bucket of water over them.

She thought back to her own parents. The affection they had shared seemed on a parallel with her feelings for Tony. On the surface they had seemed slightly indifferent to one another. Zoe couldn't remember ever seeing them hold hands or kiss impulsively. They had kissed almost as a duty every morning when her father left for work, and again when he came home each evening. Zoe had gone through a phase when she had thought they were only keeping a home going for her sake. At the time her best friend had been a girl called Sandra, whose parents had split up and were getting a divorce. Wide-eyed, Sandra had confided that her mother had gone to live with her lover. Zoe had thought her own parents were being selfless in staying together. She had romanticized it in her mind, finding it beautiful but tragic. Her mother had found her in tears once, and Zoe had explained, in her childish, halting way, that she didn't want to be the one to stand in the way of their happiness.

Her mother's eyes had filled with soft laughter. 'Oh, Zoe, my poor innocent. It's like comparing the moon with a meteorite. The moon is always there, forever constant, just like the love your father and I have for one another. The brighter meteorite burns itself out, and that's what Sandra's mother's affair with this man will do, and she'll be all alone.'

In that Zoe's mother had been right. The lover had left Sandra's mother, but by that time Sandra's father had met someone else, a gentle, smiling woman who had made Sandra a good stepmother. There was no place in his life for his former wife, so Sandra's mother had been left all alone, just as Zoe's mother had predicted. Zoe's mother had endeavored to explain it more fully. 'Your father and I have never had the bright and glittery kind of love, never been dazzled out of our senses, but that doesn't mean it isn't good. If I were to leave your father, he wouldn't last two months without me.' Her mother had been right again, her words painfully prophetic. Within two months of her mother's death, her father had gone to join her.

She must stamp Matt, and all that nonsense, out of her head. Let Camille have him.

In a quiet moment with Hannah, she couldn't help giving way to her curiosity. 'Hannah?'

'Yes, dear?'

'Monsieur Dupont's granddaughter . . . the one he speaks of so often . . .'

'Camille? What about her?'

'Is anything going on between her and

71

Matt?'

'That's something of a poser. It's always been André's dearest wish to unite our two families, and he has great respect for Matt. More to the point, Camille's always been wild about Matt. She's made no bones about that fact since she first started taking an interest in boys. Only . . . Matt isn't a boy . . . He's considerably older than Camille, which he might find a deterrent.'

'I should have thought that Matt's disinterest in marriage would be more of a deterrent.'

Hannah scoffed. 'That's a famous bachelor chant, until some enterprising female makes him swallow his words. But how did you know that about Matt?'

'I guess I must have picked it up from Tony,' Zoe replied, hastily averting her eyes. Her brain drummed on the thought that Hannah had said that Camille had always been wild about Matt. She hadn't said anything about Matt being wild about Camille.

Zoe wasn't glued to Tony's side. She explored the old town of Les Pins and the surrounding countryside on her own. Hannah had a car in the garage, a dear and faithful friend, almost in the vintage class, but she said it needed looking at, otherwise she would have been pleased to let Zoe use it to travel further afield. Zoe thanked her for the kind thought but said she wouldn't have dared to take it out

72

in any case. There wasn't a single scratch on its immaculate paintwork, and Zoe was perfectly content to accept the limits of her own legs. Several beaches within walking and busing distance beckoned tantalizingly, but Zoe resisted her preference for sunbathing within sight of the sea in order to keep Tony company, as she did one day, when they sat on adjacent loungers in Les Charmettes' small private garden.

'What do you think of Nan?' Tony inquired. 'You're not finding that she talks you to death?'

'Oh, no! I think she's wonderful. She's fascinating to listen to, although . . .'

'Yes?'

'She's very blunt. I often go hot under the collar.'

'I know the feeling all too well,' Tony said, with a dry laugh.

'But she's such a darling, I could forgive her anything.' Zoe swung her legs over the side of the lounger and stood up, looking trim yet shapely in a black one-piece swimsuit which was cut high at the thighs to show off her slender and incredibly lovely legs. 'Must make a move and get ready for dinner.'

At all other times the atmosphere was casual, but Hannah made a point of dressing for the evening meal. As she explained to Zoe, it was so easy to get sloppy and fall into bad habits when living alone. Zoe thought it was a nice custom and was glad that she had brought suitable coordinates and one long dress, at the same time realizing that she would have been pleased to ring the changes more often and wishing she'd brought more formal clothes with her.

'Give me a kiss before you go,' Tony instructed.

She leaned over and kissed him lightly on the lips. When he tried to pull her down beside him, she adeptly wriggled beyond his reach.

'You haven't gone cold on me, have you?' he inquired suspiciously.

'No, of course not.'

'I'm going to want proof of that when I get rid of these damned crutches. It seems ages since I was really close to you.

'You know I'm frightened of hurting your ribs.'

'I know. It's just that you've got a fantastic figure. I've never seen as much of it before. I'm not talking about what I want to do here and now at this particular moment. I want to do more than kiss and hold you. We would have been married now, if—'

'Have some patience, Tony.'

'I know . . . I know. It's just that you are so lovely. Sit here,' he said, patting the space beside his hip. 'I want to kiss you properly.'

'All right. But just bear in mind the lack of privacy,' she said, sitting beside him and winding her arms round his neck. Because he was in a reclining position his hands were free, and he slid them round her back, pulling her down onto his chest. Because it was unexpected, she went down harder than she would have done, and he yelped in pain. 'See what I mean, Tony? That's what I was afraid of.'

'Yes, damn it.'

'Are you all right?'

'I'm frustrated. Aren't you?'

'Yes.' Not for the first time she wondered if she was as frustrated as she ought to have been. 'I must go and get ready, otherwise I'll run the risk of being late for dinner, and you know that for this meal Hannah is a stickler for punctuality.

Not being able to argue with that undeniable truth, Tony reluctantly let her go.

Zoe luxuriated in a shower. Not only did it refresh, but it got rid of the stickiness of her sun cream. To her delight she noticed that she was beginning to acquire a tan. She would never be the color of teak, because of her fair skin, but she was extremely lucky that she didn't blister and go an unbecoming shade of red.

She hadn't worn the long dress yet. Because it was white, she had decided to save it until her skin began to brown. As she admired her new golden coloring, she realized that the time was now.

It had a bra-type top and shoestring

shoulder straps. The front was quite modest by some standards, but the back scooped down to her waist and because of this she couldn't wear a strapless bra. Going bra-less made it seem quite daring. Her new and attractive coloring deepened the sapphire blue of her eyes, which she further enhanced with a smudge of sapphire eye shadow. She brushed her hair into a bright gleaming bell and let it swing freely about her shoulders. Her very high-heeled sandals were just a collection of straps. The fact that she decided to go barelegged didn't rob her appearance of elegance. She looked cool and summery. Then she pursed her full mouth quizzically. Something else was needed—and she knew what. The pendant with the bright sapphire stone would be the perfect finishing touch. The something blue for the wedding that hadn't taken place. She hesitated for a moment, then put it on. The cold feel of it chilled her flesh, or was it the memory of Matt's fingers brushing against her skin as he'd put it on for her? Or merely too much sun? She had sunbathed longer than normal, feeling that by this time she ought to be more acclimatized. As if to prove that this was not so, a headache was beginning to pinch at her temple.

Looking at her watch as she clasped it round her wrist, she saw that she was much earlier than she had anticipated being. She had time to take a gentle stroll outside, which she felt would be beneficial.

Hannah followed the Continental trend of dining late, and the light was fast fading from the sky. A sizable chunk of the garden lay in the shadow of the house; the trees made black swathes across her path. They plunged her deeper still into the soft, fragrant obscurity. The day had burned the essence from the heart of each flower and the curl of every leaf to make a headier odor. Evening carried a more gentle scent that was like cologne to her throbbing senses.

Through the arch she spied a car's headlights as it swung to follow the curve of the drive, spotlighting her for a brief moment before going on up to the house. Visitors? She couldn't remember Hannah mentioning that she was having guests. What kind of car could it be? The lights had seemed far brighter and positioned higher than normal. She must make sure she didn't stay out overlong and make herself late for dinner. On the other hand, if there was going to be company and chatter, it seemed more essential than ever for her to clear her head.

Somewhere in the house a radio was playing. A throaty baritone was pouring the tenderness of his heart out, not that she could understand the words; the only one she could make out was *chérie.* The voice was deep and sexy, the melody soft and hauntingly romantic; the way it played on her emotions told her that it had to be a love song.

A much nearer voice, even deeper and with seductive vibrations that squeezed her throat unbearably dry, said, 'Good evening, Zoe.'

CHAPTER FOUR

'Matt!' she gasped. In his dark clothes he merged with the shadows. She couldn't see his face, but surely that was Matt's voice? For a brief moment she contested this thought, wondering if her mind was playing tricks and it was Tony. But no! Tony's approach was always heralded by the thump of his crutches. 'Matt,' she repeated weakly, and her heart began to thud. 'You . . . you startled me.'

'Sorry. My intention was to surprise, not startle. I spotted you in my headlights as I pulled into the drive.'

'It was you in that car?'

'Yes. Except that it isn't a car. It's a truck. I had a delivery to make in Marseilles. Mother is having a room prepared for me. You looked inviting standing there in your white dress. I thought I'd join you. What are you doing out here, all by yourself?'

'I have a bit of a headache. I was hoping the fresh air would clear it.'

'Been overdoing the sun?' he queried, taking a step forward, his hands going up to her neck. His thumbs rested in the hollows at her throat; his strong fingers curved to her neck and gently massaged, lifting the tight knots and taking the tension into his own fingertips. Then one hand went to the back of her neck and the other captured her chin, twisting it gently from side to side. Her neck gave a small protesting creak, then moved freely. 'That better?'

'Yes, thank you. It feels . . . wonderful.'

'You know I'm going to kiss you, don't you?'

'Please don't, Matt.'

'You don't really mean that.'

'I do. This isn't fair to Tony.'

'Are you still persisting in that nonsense?'

'If you mean am I still going to marry him, the answer is yes, as soon as it's possible. You only got the wedding delayed. You haven't put it off permanently.'

'I? I had nothing to do with getting Tony drunk, so drunk he was incapable of looking after himself and behaved like an irresponsible fool.'

'No? I know you didn't intend him to fall down those stairs, but you had a hand in the other. You encouraged him to drink more than was good for him. That's one accusation I will not withdraw. Because you did! The smirk on your face when I came round to see Tony and you told me that when you'd left him he looked as if he'd take a week to sober up is something I'll never forget. I'll never forgive you.'

'You have a vivid imagination.'

'I know you, Matt.'

'And I know you, apparently better than you know yourself. You idiot, you wouldn't be happy if you married Tony.'

'*When* I find out, I'll let you know.'

'Why you goading little . . .' The fingers still clutching her chin tightened their hold. Her chin wasn't released until his mouth was firmly planted on hers, forcing her head back with such ferocity that she thought her neck would have snapped but for the hand supporting it.

Even in the height of her indignation, she exhilarated in the sweet brutality of that kiss. No one could move her like this. She came alive for him.

When he finally released her, he said, 'You wanted that as much as I did.'

To her deep chagrin and shame, that was the undeniable truth.

'I think we'd better go in now,' he said. 'I still have to change. But first, for what it's worth, this doesn't suit me any more than it does you. You're my weakness, Zoe. I don't like it.'

'You found the strength to stay away from me for five years.'

'That's not strictly true. I tried to look you up. I drew a blank. I discovered that you'd changed your address and your job.'

'You didn't look very hard. You could have

found me if your wanted to badly enough.'

'Fair comment. It would be untrue to say I've spent all that time pining for you. But I've thought of you. That last time—well, you don't need me to tell you that things got steamy between us. I would have come back if circumstances had permitted. I admit that before that night I'd looked on you as a bit of a kid.'

'Whose head was turned by the money you flung around,' she spat angrily.

'I'm not used to people liking me for myself. I've often wondered if I would have got that far with you if I got my hands dirty by filling someone else's pocket.

'I feel sorry for you. It must be horrible to have such a jaundiced outlook.'

'Keep your sympathy. That's something I'd no intention of having then, and I won't tolerate it now.'

'What's that supposed to mean?'

'I fight fair. That's what,' he said bitterly, taking her elbow and turning her in the direction of the house.

He would have guided her straight into the room from which the sound of Hannah's and Tony's voices were coming had she not drawn away at the bottom of the stairs. 'I'd better go up and check on my lipstick before going in. I'll be like lightning.'

She was true to her word and didn't dawdle. She merely ran a comb through her hair and a lip gloss across her mouth.

Her predinner sherry was waiting for her when she got back down. She saw with relief that Hannah and Tony had only just started theirs.

'I hope I'm not holding things up?' she inquired stupidly. Obviously she wasn't. Matt wouldn't have had time to get back after changing into something more formal than the clothes he'd traveled in. Because what had happened out there in the garden was burning in her brain, she wondered how Hannah and Tony could *not* know. Which was equally ridiculous.

'Not at all. We're waiting for Matt. Even though I half expected it, it was still a wonderful surprise when he walked in, unannounced—just as I said it would be.' Hannah's quizzical eyes lifted briefly from Zoe's to look beyond her head, lighting up with affection as they did so. 'Here he is now.'

Casting Matt a cool look, Zoe crossed the room to sit by Tony's side. Somehow she had to establish her allegiance.

'Did you have a good trip down?' Tony asked. Although it was a civil enough inquiry, Zoe detected a slight edge to his voice.

'He had company,' Hannah supplied.

'That's right,' Matt verified. He seemed to be looking straight at Zoe, but she supposed that he could have been looking at Tony. 'I brought Camille with me. When I mentioned that I was coming, she asked me if I'd give her a lift.'

Zoe registered that. So he was seeing Camille.

'In the cab of the truck, mind,' Hannah said with a laugh. 'That crazy girl would ride on a shovel for Matt.'

What girl wouldn't? Zoe speculated, looking unhappily down at her hands, but not before she'd seen the amused lift of Matt's mouth, which cruelly mocked her.

As the evening progressed she wondered if either Hannah or Tony knew of the beneath-the-surface crosscurrents. The tide of feeling between her and Matt was such that it pulled her eyes until they ached in their sockets; she couldn't seem to drag her gaze from his face for any reasonable length of time. She hoped the others weren't aware of that. Hannah was full of joy at having her son there. Tony was back in top garrulous form. Strange, she had never noticed before that he talked a lot but said little. Not like Matt, who used words economically, so that when he opened his mouth everyone listened.

For what it was worth, she saw that the thing between her and Matt wasn't one way. She was conscious of Matt's eyes shifting back to her again and again. She didn't like the concentration on her lips, as if to remind her of that recent forbidden kiss. She wanted to scrub her hand across her mouth to rub out

83

the torrid memory. It didn't help her to know that his mocking amusement increased on a par with her discomfort.

It was Hannah who said, 'You're unusually quiet this evening, Zoe. Are you not feeling well?'

'Truthfully, I'm not my normal self. I think I'm paying the price of vanity.'

'You?' her hostess queried in disbelief.

'I wanted to quicken up the tanning process, so I might have sunbathed too long.'

'Ah, most unwise. You must be more careful in future.'

'One learns by one's mistakes. I intend to be.' She averted her gaze from Hannah's face to meet those compelling black eyes again. 'Will anyone mind if I break up the party? I think I'll go to bed.'

'Of course not, Zoe. I don't intend to wait too long before I turn in myself. Run along, child,' Hannah said.

'Goodnight, Hannah. Goodnight, Matt.' Zoe bent to kiss Tony. He let her and then grinned impishly as he said, 'An early night wouldn't come amiss for me, either.' He scooped up his crutches and accompanied her out of the room.

Zoe carefully closed the door behind them, glad to be out of range of Matt's vision. At the bottom of the stairs she turned. 'Goodnight again, Tony.'

'Don't go straight up. Come and look at the

stars from my bedroom window.'

He had already hinted at something like this, but this was the first time he'd come out with the direct suggestion. Odd that he'd waited until Matt's arrival to do so.

'Have you forgotten that your room happens to be right next to your grandmother's?'

'No. And neither have I forgotten that we're engaged.'

'Tony . . . I . . .'

'I know. You're feeling wretched. That's obvious just from looking at you. I can tell that you're not putting it on. I'm being inconsiderate, aren't I?'

'Well . . . I . . .' Zoe felt awful about making him feel guilty. The shame was all hers. She was horrified at her glibness in covering up. It wasn't the ultraviolet rays of the sun that were responsible for the way she felt. She had a great need to unburden herself to Tony—but what could she say? If Matt had been a secret from her past, something that was dead and buried, it would have been difficult to explain but not impossible. What made it virtually impossible was her awareness of Matt now. She couldn't very well say, 'I was infatuated with your uncle when I was a silly nineteen-year-old and knew no better—and nothing's changed, except that I'm five years older, because I'm as madly attracted to him as ever.'

Surely, when she was safely married to

Tony, everything would be all right? She pulled herself up sharply. Safely married to Tony? That sounded as though she was viewing marriage merely as a way to escape from her own weakness.

'If only I hadn't been so stupid,' Tony said, the floor receiving an aggressive thump from his crutch.

In repentance at the thought that skidded across her mind, that in one way she was glad of the enforced postponement of their wedding, Zoe slid her arms round his waist and snuggled close. Tony leaned his second crutch against the newel post to free his hand to go round Zoe and bring her closer still. He was not inexperienced. His kiss was both expert and ardent. When it kindled no answering response in her she told herself fiercely that it was because she wasn't in the mood. There was a light in his eyes which told her that he was—very much so. He was still hankering for her to go to his room with him.

Very firmly she said, 'Goodnight, Tony.'

She knew she was falling short of what he had a right to expect from his fiancée, and the disappointment on his face made her heart ache slightly.

He crooked a finger under her chin, and this time his kiss gave warm pleasure and asked nothing of her. 'Goodnight, Zoe.'

She turned and went up the stairs. Not until she rounded the curve and was out of his sight

86

did she hear the thud of his crutches as he made his way to his room.

She sat on the bed meditating for endless moments. It was quite a while before she kicked off her sandals and reached her arms up round her neck to unfasten her pendant—and discovered that she was no longer wearing it. Oh, no! Her distress as she wondered when she could have lost it was acute, and disproportionate. It was no good trying to fool herself that her torment wasn't because Matt had given it to her.

She knew she wouldn't be able to sleep until she'd tried to find it. She slid her feet back into her sandals and retraced her steps downstairs. There was no sign of it anywhere on the stairs, or in the downstairs rooms, which were now also empty of the other occupants. Obviously everyone had decided to follow her lead and go to bed.

She knew that she had definitely put the pendant on before coming down the first time, but now that she thought about it she couldn't remember seeing it round her neck when she went up again to retouch her makeup after that encounter with Matt in the garden. Of course! She remembered—rather too vividly for her peace of mind—the way Matt had massaged and manipulated her neck to ease her headache. That's when it must have come loose.

She let herself out the door and followed

the path she had taken earlier, stopping at the spot where she had stood with Matt.

'We'll have to stop meeting like this,' a voice said.

'Matt!' She swung round, shrieking his name in frustration at the ill fate that had brought about this second confrontation. 'What are you doing here?'

'Taking a much-needed breath of air. Thinking what a pity it was I wasn't sharing the moment with a suitable companion . . . and here *you* are,' he said with dry mockery.

'I didn't come in search of you, if that's what you're thinking.'

'No?'

'No. I've lost my pendant. The one you bought me to wear for the wedding . . . for my wedding to Tony,' she emphasized. 'I was wearing it earlier this evening. I thought it might be here, so I came to look.'

'I'd suggest that we look for it together, except that in this light it might be a bit like looking for a needle in a haystack. Not being a smoker, I carry neither a cigarette lighter nor matches. But I'm forgetting; knowing the mission you were on, you would have come better prepared.'

'No, I . . . I didn't think,' she said, dropping to her knees and combing the ground with her fingers, feeling foolish and angry. Foolish because she hadn't thought to come equipped with a flashlight, and angry with him for what he obviously thought—for his arrogant assumption in thinking that she had seen him leave the house from her bedroom window, which did happen to look out on this part of the garden, and had made up the excuse of losing her pendant so she could follow him.

He bent to take an elbow in each hand and eased her back up. 'It's useless, Zoe. If it's here, it will come to no harm. I promise to look for it for you first thing in the morning.'

'It *is* here. At least'—she bit her lip—'I don't know that for certain, but it's possible that it may be.'

'Yes, yes, of course.'

'Stop humoring me. Why won't you believe me?'

'I do believe you, Zoe.'

'I'm being honest about this,' she insisted.

'So am I. Honest in admitting that we're two of a kind.'

'What do you mean by that?'

'We both like playing with fire.'

'You might. I don't,' she denied.

'Come off it. You were playing with fire when you got entangled with Tony.

'What are you talking about? And I'm not entangled with Tony. That sounds insulting. I'm engaged to him.'

'Yes. And I'm wondering why. Why you ever looked at him in the first place. In case you feel coy about enlarging on that, I'll do it for you. You knew that it would eventually lead you back to me. I don't believe that Tony's chief attractions were his good looks and boyish charm. What drew you to him was his relationship to me. Did you get involved with him—I'll say involved, as you seem ill at ease with the word "entangled"—to get back at me? Or back *with* me? Which, Zoe? You knew that at some time or another we would be bound to meet again through him—in circumstances much like this.'

'I've never heard anything so ridiculous in all my life,' she said, her voice shrill with indignation. 'I was attracted to Tony for himself from the beginning. The one drawback was his close relationship to you. I thought he might turn out to be as horrid as you are. Thankfully, that fear has so far proved to be groundless. Tony's manner has always been kind and gracious, his behavior impeccable. I couldn't wish for a gentler, more considerate, or more understanding fiancé.'

'Kind, gracious, gentle, considerate . . . you make him sound like a milksop. Are those the qualities you really want in a husband? As for understanding, that's a laugh. You found him so understanding that you couldn't bring yourself to tell him that his own uncle had very nearly been there first.'

'How crude. Have you thought that I might not have said anything out of consideration for you? Assuming that Tony has some respect for you, perhaps I didn't want to destroy it. You've had a lot of fun in the past in telling me that you were too much of a man for me. You've asked for this, Matt Hunter. Would a man of honor have behaved as you did?'

'You were nineteen. That's not such a child.' Despite that, she knew by the tone of his voice that she had got to him, that he didn't like to think that he'd taken unfair advantage.

There was a stiffness about his shoulders that told of the fury he was desperately trying to suppress. He half turned, and for a moment she thought he was going to walk away. It was that supposition that held her motionless and made her an easy target for the arms that came round her, bringing her body up close to his. She was too taken by surprise to protest, and then his mouth was on hers, hard and sweet, draining the desire to do so, firing her blood with a contrary craving for the kiss never to end.

She knew that she didn't have the physical strength to free herself. If she was to gain her release it had to be by other means. The best her spinning brain could come up with was to be a rag doll in his arms, and so she fought to keep her responses in check. She must not let him know how exquisitely he brought her to life. She played dead, her arms remaining by her sides, her lips tightly compressed to shut him out. She had no control over the fast beating of her heart, the thudding pulse his lips came down on as they moved briefly to her temple before returning to possess her mouth. That hardly mattered. That wildness wasn't a giveaway; it could easily be taken for anger.

But it came to her that she was fighting a desperate, losing battle. Because he believed that she had come out on a pretext, that this was what she really wanted, he battered her resistance down degree by subtle degree. When his initial ardent assault failed to achieve its object, the hands binding her to his hips unlocked their steely grip, throwing the emotions pounding beneath the cool façade she was still valiantly trying to preserve into wild disorder. One tangled in her hair; the other drew circles of fire over her shoulder blades before descending along the bumpy column of her spine to her waist. His light, seductive fingerplay teased the entire area of flesh exposed by the low cut of her dress; then his mouth brushed hers, an insouciant feather touch that left her wanting him to show her his former depth of passion. Devious Matt. Because when that passion returned it was greeted with a welcoming moan, a sigh that rose tremulously from a throat that arched of its own volition to accept his kiss.

She melted against him as his lips turned hers to fire, destroying her last defense. Her arms wound helplessly round his lean waist as the scorching passion burnt through her mouth to her mind, igniting her nerve ends and sending a fierce throb of delight through her body. At the same time the intensity of her own desire made itself known as a physical ache that wouldn't be evicted until it had been appeased.

She tasted the salt tears of shame at the back of her throat and recklessly swallowed them back. All that mattered was the pleasure he was giving her as his lips alternately crushed and treasured hers and his hands adored and delighted her receptive flesh. His finger stroked down from her cheek, outlined her jaw, and came down her throat and along her collarbone, pausing to hook under her shoulder strap and bring it down her arm.

He groaned. 'The low back of your dress has driven me crazy all evening . . . wondering.'

'And now you know,' she said, her voice going husky as he traced a delicate line over the upper swell before his hand closed fully over her naked breast.

Expectation hardened the rosy bud even before it knew the abrasive ecstasy of his gently rotating fingers. She sobbed her love moans into his neck, her teeth nipping his flesh, expressing her joy and inciting a more ardent, less delicate caress. It was inflammatory. Her lashes dropped over her passion-glazed eyes, and she sighed as his lips glided silkily down her throat, covering it with molten fire as he tasted her skin, slowly and methodically, savoring every inch of the tantalizingly slow descent until his mouth took the tingling tip of her breast into custody and the molten fire swept lower as her stomach curled up in intense sexual excitement.

'You're so warm and desirable.' His voice shivered against her hairline for a brief moment before her head was driven back by an explosive, exploring kiss that was almost an act of possession in itself.

The hand low on her back locked them together, but even without that her compulsion to be near to him would have held her there. The rock-hard masculinity of his body, his vigor and his strength were as exciting as they were tantalizing. She had thought that only men fantasized, that lust was strictly a male prerogative, something that was not to be entertained by a nicely brought up woman. A man had to have a woman to fulfill a physical necessity; a woman gave herself out of love. But it wasn't always so, she realized in that exhilarating moment. She wanted Matt as intensely as she knew that he wanted her. She imagined what it would be like to be this close to him without the barrier of clothes, to lie with him hip to hip and drown in bliss in his arms. Why not? . . .

With slow precision he brought her shoulder strap back up again. His arm curved round the back of her waist as he walked her out from beneath the canopy of trees. When they moved out of the shade, the stars seemed to her to be particularly luminous. The night was magic. The warm scented air stroked her skin, shivering it with remembered sensations. Every place that Matt's roving hands had touched was still astir with feeling; all sorts of frenzied activity seemed to be going on just below the surface of her skin.

Zoe could have reached her bedroom via the outside staircase and long balcony, but she automatically went into the house with Matt, who locked up and put out the lights.

'I'm just down the passage from you,' he said as they went up the stairs together.

'Oh.' She had wondered.

There was a question in his eyes which she didn't have the answer for. The little, yet so big, 'Why not?' haunted her mind, pinched her senses, the backs of her eyes, accelerated her heartbeat, and made breathing a challenge. Then suddenly the pinching feeling at the backs of her eyes became a humiliation of tears. She knew why not. Of all the many becauses, one should have jumped instantly into her mind. In fact, the haunting 'Why not?' should never have entered her mind in the first place because of it. She lifted her hand to her face, scraping her ring across her cheek, digging the sharp edge of the diamond cluster into it as punishment. *Because she was engaged to Tony.*

Matt didn't miss that very revealing gesture. The question left his eyes to be replaced by an unattractive smile of arrogance and contempt that mocked her self-denial. Arrogance because he knew how severely tempted she had been, how much she hadn't wanted the incident to end with merely a kiss, and the contempt possibly for the same reason. He didn't look as though he was suffering. It hurt as much as anything that he didn't seem all that bothered that he wouldn't be coming in with her.

'Pity about the pendant. I shouldn't lose any sleep over it if I were you. I'm sure it will turn up,' he scoffed.

'I'm sure it will,' she retorted. 'Most likely in the garden, where I said I'd lost it.'

'Are you quite certain you were wearing it this evening?'

'Of course I am. I distinctly remember putting it on.'

'I suppose you know best. The odd thing is, I can't recall seeing it round your neck.'

'Well, it was there, I assure you. I know what you're getting at, but you're way off the mark. I didn't make up the story of losing my pendant as an excuse to join you. I *have* lost it.' She opened her door, meaning to fling herself haughtily through it and slam it in his grinning face. Only a glint of gold and a flash of sapphire held her motionless.

Matt walked past her, crossed over to the dressing table where the pendant lay, and picked it up.

'How did it get there?' Zoe gasped

incredulously. 'I put it on. I know I did,' she said in angry exasperation.

'Perhaps you lost it before you came down. Obviously it couldn't have jumped from the floor, where it must have fallen, to the dressing table. So, say Yvette came in—to turn down the bed or something or other—and saw it lying on the floor; naturally she would pick it up and put it on the dressing table for you to find.'

'Yes, that's what must have happened,' Zoe said, grasping eagerly at the explanation.

'To make that fit, the clasp would have to be loose, wouldn't you agree?'

'I agree,' she said savagely, hating the way he was testing her. 'Look at it for yourself.'

'Thank you. It would have been ungallant to do so without your permission. Mm, let me see.' It was a spring clasp and from where Zoe stood, when he snapped it shut it seemed to be secure. 'No . . .' The hateful mockery was back in his eyes. 'It seems to be okay. It is pretty. I must say, I do have good taste.' But as he spoke he wasn't looking at the pendant. His eyes scintillated over her face.

He handed it back to her, and she examined the clasp for herself. It was perfectly all right. When she'd put it on her thoughts had gone naturally to Matt because he had given it to her, and she'd been agitated because of that. She couldn't have been attentive enough to what she was doing and so she hadn't fastened it properly, but nothing would convince Matt that she hadn't told him a lie to explain why she joined him in the garden.

'Think what you like,' she said aggressively, 'only just get out.'

He took hold of her jaw. His thumb lay in the indentation between her chin and lower lip before stroking along its softly curving fullness. 'You don't need an excuse, Zoe. Whatever the time, wherever I am, if the urge takes you, just come.'

With that he sauntered out, leaving Zoe choking on anger, humiliation, shame, and frustration.

CHAPTER FIVE

How could she have stayed out with Matt, let him kiss and caress her the way he had? She felt ashamed that she had succumbed to something that was purely physical, nothing more than lust. Something that couldn't last. She had been hurt once; now she was leaving herself wide open to be hurt all over again. She believed Matt when he said he'd tried to look her up but had failed because she'd changed her job and moved to a new address. But the excuse lost all its value when she recalled that she'd been at her old job and former home for three years after he'd walked out before she'd decided to make a change. For heaven's sake, he'd had three years to come back to her! That was how interested he'd been.

His interest had only really perked up when he discovered that she was going to marry Tony; then he'd jumped in quickly to stake his claim and try to break them up. It was terrible to think that he only wanted her because someone else did, but she couldn't come up with anything better.

In letting Matt get close to her again, it wasn't only a second dose of hurt she was inviting; there was something else. Could she honestly contemplate letting a decent man like Tony go, a solid man who would give her a good and durable marriage, in favor of some short-term sparkle? It was true that Tony was still Matt's paler reflection, lacking his strength of character, but he was young yet, only a year older than she was herself. In another ten years, who knew but that he wouldn't match up to Matt in every way.

Her thoughts ran back to the accusation that Matt had flung at her, about playing with fire when she got involved with Tony, saying that she had only been drawn to Tony because she had hoped Tony would lead her back to him. She had denied that emphatically, but had she been right to do so?

She might have been attracted to Tony because he looked a lot like Matt, but that was another matter entirely and totally acceptable.

People did tend to go for the same kind of looks and coloring in their search for a partner. Women were said to have a preference for men who resembled their fathers. Her father had been dark-haired, like Matt and Tony. And fair-haired men had never appealed to her much.

She found herself harping again on Matt's debasing allegation that she had only encouraged Tony because she'd thought the relationship would bring her in contact with Matt again. She couldn't shrug it off; she wasn't going to have any peace of mind until she'd worried it through to the end. It was as distasteful to her as thinking that Matt only wanted her now because Tony did, yet she couldn't say there was no truth in it, even if only at a subconscious level. It cast her in a most unfavorable light; she wouldn't have thought herself capable of such underhanded dealing. But that apart, was it something to bother about? Even if Matt *had* been on her mind when she had first encountered Tony, she had come to like and love Tony for himself, and surely that was all that mattered.

Love was gentle and caring. Infatuation could outshine it every time. She had to be strong about this. She couldn't let the feelings she experienced with Matt dazzle her out of her senses, blind her to something precious and lasting. Nature could be very cruel. In the same way that the brightest and most attractive berries were often poisonous, it wasn't fair that something so beautiful, that gave her life a special sparkle, should be a sham.

*   *   *

The next morning Zoe woke up to another beautiful day. She pulled on her lightweight cotton robe, flung open the door leading out onto the long balcony, and stepped outside, as had been her custom since her arrival.

There wasn't a cloud in the burning blue sky. This early in the morning she would have been shivering back home, even on England's hottest day. This air was blissfully warm, clear, and light, with a strange luminosity that Zoe was only just getting used to and that brought the colors more vividly to life. It was like taking off smoky glasses and seeing a richness of foliage that she had never imagined. She could never have believed that there were so many shades of green or that red could be so red. The sun-saturated stone of the buildings ranged from glaring white to a glowing, living gold and hurt eyes that were unaccustomed to it.

She was lucky enough to be enjoying a holiday on the French Riviera. She had a wonderful hostess and a kind and compatible fiancé. Was she going to let all this be spoiled for her by the dark intrusion of a figure from

101

her past who had no place at all in her current well-ordered life?

The unmistakable fragrance of coffee hit her a second before Matt's deep voice announced, 'Good morning, Zoe. I knew instinctively that you would be an early riser, and I had the forethought to instruct Yvette to bring a spare cup. Come and have breakfast with me.'

Zoe choked on her despair. The past she was so valiantly trying to deny was too forcefully in the present for her liking. A memory was easier to stamp out than a living, mocking reminder. She had forgotten that, as Matt had a room farther along the passage from hers, he would also be sharing the balcony. Monique and Pierre were also on their level, so it wasn't as if they were completely isolated, but the old couple's quarters were at the back of the house. Sharing a balcony with Matt was an intimacy she could have done without.

'I haven't brushed my teeth yet,' she said.

A dark eyebrow arched in cruel amusement at the flimsiness of that excuse for not sharing his table. 'Then run along and brush your teeth, if you must. But hurry, or the coffee will get cold.'

She nodded mutely but remained rooted to the spot. Her leaden feet somehow wouldn't obey the command of her brain. She didn't so much want to run along and do his bidding as run away. But running away had never solved anything. It would be unrealistic to go ahead and marry Tony while there was the tiniest suspicion of Matt's dark shadow lurking in her heart. She must face up to him and somehow push him out, not let him affect her in this way. She didn't feel very proud of herself. It was shallow to let Matt move her as he did.

He was already dressed in the second-skin jeans he'd been wearing the morning she'd called to see Tony. Standing there, unable to move, devouring him with her eyes and not being able to do a thing about it, she felt skinned, her jumping nerve ends, the warmth of her feelings for him, exposed for his cruel observation. To complement the jeans he wore a sky blue shirt that flapped open and showed off that tantalizing V of tightly curling hair. Her fingertips still prickled as she wondered if it would be coarse or silky to the touch.

His smile slashed deeper and more mockingly, as if he had intercepted that thought, and that gave her the impetus to move.

She brushed her teeth and rinsed her face. She combed her hair but decided to remain in the cotton robe, which gave adequate, demure coverage and allowed her to be back in a minimum of time. She didn't want him to think that she was nervous at returning to be in his company, or that she was taking her time to doll up for him.

As well as the coffee, there were orange juice, croissants, and a cherry preserve that Zoe pronounced as delicious on taking the first bite.

After demolishing his roll Matt reached out to the flat basket where the hot croissants were piled on a snow-white napkin, transferring one to his plate and covering it with a large portion of the preserve. This task done, he inquired lazily, 'What were you thinking about earlier to put that look on your face?'

'What look?' she asked carefully, feeling a painful prickling in her cheeks.

'Before I made my presence known you were lost to the world—just staring as if you'd never seen a blade of grass, a tree, or a flower before.'

She smiled, softening toward him. For a moment she'd thought he was referring to the way she had looked at him. There must have been some kindness in him that he had mentioned one and not the other. 'It's as if I never have seen any of those things before, at least not in their true perspective. I don't quite know how to put. this, but a kind of wonder hit me, as if . . .' Her brow furrowed in concentration. 'Perhaps this sounds crazy. I've never been in a hospital and had a serious operation, the kind you don't know if you're going to come out of in one piece or not. But every morning when I wake up I have to rush out and stand on this balcony. The feeling I get is as though I've just come out of a deep anesthetic which I went into not knowing if I would ever see this lovely world clearly again, and when I come out I appreciate it more than ever, and it's better than ever. I rub the blur of sleep from my eyes and I can't believe the clarity of things, the brilliance of the colors and the sharpness of the focus. Can you understand at all what I'm getting at?'

She couldn't understand why it was important for him to know what she meant any more than she understood why the silence before he answered was like a cold finger touching her heart. There were many kinds of silences. Thinking silences. Golden sharing silences. Silences that hummed as sweetly as a song. And ominous silences that carried some deep dread warning. And no silence she had ever encountered before had been as ominous as this one.

'Yes, I do.' The warmth on his face was replaced by bitter understanding. For a moment, a moment so brief that she could have imagined it and probably had, because she couldn't think what she had said to put him out, his face was a carved mask, except for the living pain in his eyes. His heavy lids dropped. When they lifted he was wearing another mask, one that was all too familiar. He had on the mocking, taunting look which she had come to hate and wanted to scratch away with her long fingernails. Scratch it to the bone and never have to see it again. 'What are you considering doing today? Or haven't you got any plans except to sit and hold your fiancé's hand?'

'I happen to find Tony's company enchanting; I like to be with him. But I've never been to this part of the world before, so it's natural that I should want to do some exploring. And that's what I'm going to do today. Tony is very unselfish about it. He can't accompany me, but he doesn't stop me from going out.'

'I take the hint. Unfortunately, I've got other things to do today. Sorry about that,' he drawled.

'I didn't mean—' She frowned, biting heavily on her lip. He had read something in her words which she had never intended. She didn't want his company. She would rather dance all day with a snake than spend five minutes alone with him! Yet what had she meant, if she hadn't been angling for Matt to take her somewhere?

Back in her room, her simmering anger cooling as she took her morning shower and considered what to do, she told herself firmly, almost convincingly, that if she had wanted Matt to take her somewhere it was for his services as a guide and not for his infinitely disrupting presence. She supposed she could have bought this service by taking a conducted. tour. But although she was a born tourist, delighting in walking medieval ramparts, snapping her camera at Roman ruins, and generally reveling in antiquities, she didn't like to go in a crowd or to the fashionable places and tourist traps, preferring to wander off the beaten track on the whim of the moment.

Looking delectably cool in an easy-to-wear, lemon-ice shirtwaist dress and a large cartwheel sun hat, Zoe went to seek Tony out and let him know her intentions.

He was reclining in his usual lounger in the garden; it was positioned by a small, ornamental fountain, and she felt a rush of compassion for him, because even though he was lucky to have such a fantastic spot to rest up in, and he was getting more adept at getting around on his crutches, it was still sad that he couldn't swim off one of the incredibly lovely beaches or take advantage of the surrounding countryside.

'If you don't want me to go for a walk, I'll stay with you,' she volunteered.

'No, take your walk. You look . . . sort of restless. Is anything wrong, Zoe?'

'No.'

'There is,' he persisted.

'Yes, there is,' she acknowledged. 'Actually, that's why I want to get away for a while—to think.'

'Not having second thoughts about us?' he asked with such anxiety in his eyes that it squeezed her heart.

107

'No, Tony. But when I tell you what I should have told you when we first started going out together, you might have second thoughts and want to break it off.'

He lifted a finger and placed it across her mouth. 'I don't want to hear your guilty confession . . . presumably about the men in your life before you met me. You're not nineteen anymore. It would be downright stupid of me to think there hadn't been someone before, or . . . other things. I don't much care whether you have or you haven't, or who the man is, providing it's dead and in the past. I don't want your past, just your future. So you don't have to tell me a thing.'

'That's very generous of you, Tony. Why did you choose the age of nineteen? Why didn't you say eighteen or twenty or twenty-one? Why nineteen?'

'I don't know. It was just an age I picked on. Why the fuss about that?'

'I'm not fussing. It's just that I was nineteen when I knew him.'

'What have I just told you?' he chided gently.

'You said you didn't want to know if it was dead and in the past. I want to be very honest about this, Tony. I owe you that. It's not in the past; it's turned up to haunt me.' She lowered her head to hide her eyes, which were filled with the painful truth. 'If something can haunt you it isn't dead.'

'I see.'

'How can you see?' she said, irritated by his placid acceptance and calm understanding. 'You don't know who the man is! Do you?' she challenged.

It was odd the way he took his time in replying. He either knew or he didn't know. Perhaps he wasn't as unruffled as she thought; perhaps underneath his façade of calm he was seething and wanted to take her by the shoulders and give her a good shake and was fighting to control himself and his tone.

'No, I don't know,' he said eventually.

'It's Matt.' She looked him squarely in the eye. 'I owe you an apology. I should have told you at the beginning. I didn't because I didn't think we would get serious, and then when we did, it was too late. And you didn't seem, all that friendly with Matt, despite working for him. So I foolishly let things ride.'

'You said it isn't dead. What do you mean by that?'

'Matt is a very physical man. When I saw him again, I felt the old pull. If you still want me, I'll need your understanding and your support to fight it.'

'*If* I still want you!' Just for a moment there was a bright gleam of triumph in his eyes that sickened her. It was as if he was crowing over his victory, but then the look faded into one of incredulity. 'You're saying that you'll stick with me in preference to Matt?'

'Yes, that's what I'm saying.'

'You sound very sure.'

'I am. And I'll tell you why. I want to get it all off my conscience. I was heartbroken when Matt left me five years ago.' She hated saying anything against Matt, but her first loyalty had to be to Tony if she was going to carry this through. 'It was cruel the way he finished it between us. He had a big haulage job on the Continent. He promised to get in touch with me the moment he got back. He didn't. He left me in suspense, wondering, without a word.'

'You didn't get a whiff of anything? No possible hint why?'

'What makes you ask that?' Zoe questioned, puzzled. Perhaps there was a reason, after all, something that Tony knew about, and when he told her it would clear everything up, somehow making things right.

It was a fragile hope to pin her future on, and it splintered as Tony said in a funny, strained voice, 'I just wondered, that's all. Why do you suppose he acted like that?'

She shrugged away her keen disappointment. 'Who knows? Perhaps he met someone else. Or it just came to him that I bored him.'

'His bad taste is my good fortune. I'll make you happy as he never could. You wouldn't be happy with someone you couldn't trust. You'd always wonder if he'd do the same thing again.'

'That's very true. I phoned the depot, you know.'

'Did you? No, I didn't. How could I?' he said, a slight edge to his voice.

'The woman who answered insisted on knowing my name before she'd answer my inquiry about Matt.' She laughed wryly. 'I had this stupid notion that he might have been involved in an accident and couldn't contact me. But when I told her my name she said in a very icy voice, "I'm sorry, Miss Fortune, but I am instructed to say that Mr. Hunter is not available."' She swallowed back her hurt and gripped Tony's hand. 'I think you're being fantastic about this. I couldn't blame you if you booted me out at this very moment.'

'I've no intention of doing that. I'm going to marry you. You don't know what that will mean to me. Now, go for your walk, darling. Why not ask Monique to pack you a picnic lunch, then you won't have to hurry back.' He indicated the lounger next to his. 'I'll save your place for when you get back.'

Having a place saved for her sounded warm and reliable to Zoe. 'M'm, I like the idea of a picnic lunch'. The response was light, despite the heaviness of her heart.

The hard, triumphant glimmer which Zoe had caught a brief glance of returned to Tony's eyes, belying the softness of his tone as he said, 'Enjoy your walk, darling.' But having already turned to go back into the house, Zoe didn't see it. As she paused to turn and wave, the correct smile was back in place.

*   *   *

Zoe walked in a circle, arriving at the meandering old part of the town by way of a small promenade with a pebbly beach on one side and pavement cafés on the other. The cafés attracted more locals than tourists, the latter being more inclined to head for the livelier spots. An older Frenchman with a brown weathered face and the type of beret favored by the older generation of locals winked at her and surreptitiously followed her progress. A younger, quite attractive Frenchman ogled her openly. She had thought about stopping for a coffee but decided against it when she saw that she might have company. Two men in her life provided more than enough complications. Instead she sat for an enjoyable while on the low harbor wall, watching the softly breaking water wash across the white pebbles and the aquamarine ripples made by the rhythmic bobbing of the fishing boats. The whispering slap and splash was oddly soothing. The same kind of charm and serenity and timelessness was to be found in the old town with its winding, narrow streets and high, shuttered windows.

She climbed out of town and up a zigzag path through a resinous pine forest, punishing

112

her legs with the effort as if to pay for any pain she might have caused Tony. She wouldn't have believed that anyone could be so kindly and understanding. Not one word of recrimination had crossed his lips. All that had seemed to concern him was the fact that she wasn't leaving him for Matt. He must love her very much, more than she'd thought, and it made her treatment of him seem shabby by comparison.

It was good to stamp her frustration out on the ground. She realized that she had taken an erratic course, but when she finally looked down from her vantage point above the treetops to a vista that varied from wild to cultivated to luxurious, and all of it beautiful, she knew that the experience far outweighed the odd blister and aching muscle. To get a wider view of the coastline, which was crammed with resorts and campgrounds wherever the smallest beach existed, she would need to attain considerably more height. Even if time had permitted that, her legs weren't up to it.

She found a shady spot to sit and eat her picnic lunch, which consisted of chicken, cheese, rolls, and fruit, and which she washed down with a bottle of mineral water. She remained there for quite some time, thinking, not about her decision, she'd made that, just wondering how she could cope. Matt was poison, yet she was drawn to him. How could she keep his hands off her when she yearned for his touch?

The sizzling gold of the sun was a softer shade of liquid honey that slanted obliquely over the countryside as she made her way back, her footsteps dragging with an odd reluctance.

As she proceeded up the drive to Les Charmettes she almost tripped over Matt, literally. Her view of him was at first limited to two denim clad legs protruding from beneath Hannah's car. She didn't want him to see her, she couldn't have borne another confrontation at that moment, so she moved with stealth. Her step was quieter than the leaves whispering in the trees with the wind that had risen and that plucked mischievously at the hem of her dress.

Whether he'd finished his task or just somehow sensed her presence, she had no way of knowing, but suddenly he came out from beneath the car, causing her heart to race with a peculiar rhythm at the sight of his muscled chest and brawny shoulders. A moment's contemplation would have told her that of course he would have removed his shirt to save it from getting greased up, but all that rippling vitality, coming so unexpectedly, was almost too much to take. She had known that he wasn't a sitting-behind-the-desk kind of boss and he needed to be powerfully built to handle the heavy juggernauts he drove, but knowing and *seeing* were different matters entirely.

By the time she regained her breath he had wormed his way out and was sitting cross-legged, looking up at her. He looked hot and oily, but a happy smile of accomplishment was on his face as he said, 'Hi!'

'Hi!' The wind was having another go at her skirt, and she tried to anchor it without seeming to be doing so. She wished he'd get up. The level of his view was rather off-putting.

He remained complacently where he was. 'That should do it. Had a good day?'

'Yes.' Nodding her head toward the car, she said, 'Seems apparent that you have, too.'

'I'm satisfied. I've got some work to do tomorrow. But I just may have it licked.'

He scooped up a rag to wipe his face, which looked even dirtier than his hands, if that were possible, then finally levered himself to his feet.

He was still grinning like a Cheshire cat about something. Could it be because of the satisfaction of a job well done, or something else? She was betting heavily on the something else. And she didn't think the amount of leg he'd seen, or her embarrassment in showing it, merited such amusement.

She wasn't kept in suspense for long. No longer than it took to walk past Matt, through the arch and into the garden. She stopped. The place that Tony had said he would save for her was very decoratively occupied and that some of it wasn't because of a tiny stirring of jealousy. No, she was being too hard on herself. And yet . . . She had always thought that she had a reasonably nice figure, slender but quite curvy, but the full richness of this girl's breasts made hers look like nothing. The curve of her hips was only a mite less impressive than the length and lusciousness of her legs. It came to Zoe that she was looking at the girl as a man would, figure before face, and with a sinking feeling she knew that this was because she wanted to see her through Matt's and Tony's eyes.

Zoe's breath caught again on viewing the girl's face. Her loveliness was something impossible to describe without using hackneyed metaphors. Her face was angelic, her skin perfectly smooth, its color confirming what had already been deduced from her body, that she was a sunseeker. She had a full and deeply sensuous mouth, gray eyes, thickly and darkly lashed, and silky ebony hair, and she was exuding a heavy perfume that seemed to be an intrinsic part of her. In a way she seemed old for one so young, because Zoe gauged her to be younger than herself. Somewhere between nineteen and twenty-one. The rose— no, she was too exotic a being to be likened to a rose—the flower, whatever it was, had lost its dew.

Tony struggled up from his reclining

position. It wasn't until he awkwardly moved his arm that it crossed Zoe's mind to wonder if he had been holding the girl's hand until she herself came into view. Or was the abashed look on his face because of the proximity of the two loungers—Zoe's, which the beauty had annexed, had been placed cozily close, and she hadn't bothered to push it away to create a distance between them.

Matt was still behind her, but she could feel his eyes boring into the back of her neck as he performed the necessary introduction.

'Zoe, this is Camille. Camille is the granddaughter of André Dupont, you may recall. Camille, meet Zoe, Tony's fiancée and our house guest.'

Camille made a token gesture of inclining her chin. Obviously the friendly French greeting of a kiss on each cheek was not the order of the day, at least not where Zoe was concerned. Camille might well have been less inhibited with Matt and Tony. Zoe made a similar acknowledgment, and sank gratefully back onto the lounger Matt had drawn up for her. She was mesmerized by Camille's eyes. Not for their indisputable beauty but for one other indisputable fact. Zoe looked into them and knew that her first assessment had been right. Camille's years might pronounce her to be a girl, but she was a woman. Her innocence had gone. Who had taken that look which says a girl is untouched and replaced it with worldly knowledge? Zoe wondered.

'Are you enjoying your visit here, Miss . . .? I'm sorry, but Matt did not say what your last name was,' Camille apologized.

'It's Fortune, but please call me Zoe, unless you would prefer me to call you Mademoiselle Dupont?'

'No, Camille, please.'

'I'm enjoying my visit very much, Camille. But who wouldn't be happy in these beautiful surroundings? Let me congratulate you on your excellent English.' It was better than excellent, it was fascinating when spoken with that intriguing French accent. Fascinating, and very sexy.

'I live and work in your country. I, too, am here for a visit.'

'Of course, I'm forgetting,' Zoe said, though she had forgotten no such thing. Hadn't Camille traveled down with Matt in the cab of his truck? She wasn't likely to forget that.

Matt took a clean handkerchief from his pocket, carefully shook it out, and placed it on the edge of Zoe's chair to protect it from his grimy jeans, then he perched there. Had he done that to be near her or because that angle gave him a better view of the delectable Camille?

Because Matt was in a much worse state than she was, Zoe hadn't felt disheveled when talking to him. But now, in the presence of Mademoiselle Cool and Composed, she felt decidedly grubby. She was hot and weary, her flat-heeled sandals carried the white dust of the path she'd followed, and she yearned to sink her aching limbs into a reviving bath before they seized up. Not to mention the fact that her hair had been blown to kingdom come by the wind. Perhaps it was as well that neither Matt nor Tony was looking at her, because she couldn't bear the comparison.

They chatted for a while about this and that. Then Camille stretched with catlike grace, but not, Zoe felt, because she needed to stretch, but because the action showed off her stunning figure. 'I could sit here forever,' she said. 'It's so pleasant. But I must drag myself away.'

'Won't you stay for dinner?' Matt invited.

She pulled a face at him. '*Chéri,* if only I could. Papa is having guests. It is a masculine affair. A reunion. He asked me explicitly to be there to welcome them. I shall be terribly bored, but I cannot do anything about it. Now'—her worldly eyes darted mischievously from Matt to Tony—'which of you gallant gentlemen is going to walk me home?'

As Tony shrugged and looked helplessly at his leg, Matt rose obligingly. 'Give me a few moments to wash and put a shirt on.'

Camille used the time to slip into the sundress which she had discarded and flung over the back of her chair. It was a bright poppy red. Respectably dressed, but looking every bit as alluring, she said, 'I'll go say goodbye to your grandmother, Tony. Goodbye for now, Zoe. I hope we meet again very soon.'

'I hope so, too,' Zoe responded. The lie sounded hollow even to herself.

CHAPTER SIX

Soon after that Zoe excused herself to take her long awaited soak and change for dinner. There was no sign of either Matt or Camille, she observed on entering the house, but Hannah smiled a welcome at her.

'I'm glad you got back from your walk in time to meet Camille. What do you think of her? Don't you find her a delightful child?'

'Child?' Zoe queried, irony in her voice.

'Ah—yes! French girls mature more quickly, but Camille is only nineteen.'

'I thought she might be, although I would have taken her for older.'

'Was she flirting too outrageously with Tony? Is that why you're on edge? Little French girls flutter their eyelashes from the crib. They practice on their papas, but they quickly realize what it's all about and transfer their attention to the nearest unrelated male. Both Matt and Tony were suitable candidates, since they spent long vacations with me. It's almost a way of life for Camille to flaunt herself before them. It is naughty, I admit, but then, Camille has always been inclined to be a little naughty. She has been spoiled. André worships her and has never been able to say *non* where she is concerned. But I assure you that what she does means nothing. Satisfied?'

'Yes. Thanks for explaining it to me,' Zoe said, wondering if Hannah really believed her own propaganda.

It was no coincidence that Zoe took special pains with her appearance that evening, selecting from her limited wardrobe a long, multicolored skirt with delicate silver thread running through it. Because of its many colors she could ring the changes with a variety of tops, but she discarded the black one she usually wore and chose a silver top with narrow straps. Even though she couldn't hope to measure up to Camille, she looked stunning and she knew it, and additional confidence came from knowing that Camille wouldn't be alongside for comparison.

Because she had taken rather longer than normal, she had no time for her usual stroll in the garden. Although there was no sign yet of Hannah, Zoe knew that Matt and Tony were in the dining room because she could hear their voices. She halted as she realized that they weren't involved in a normal conversation and withdrew her hand from the doorknob. Unless she was very much mistaken, they were in the middle of an angry discussion about something.

She heard Tony say, 'Can't you get it into your head that she's chosen me? You're out of the running, Matt. Why are you trying to foul it up for me?'

'Foul it up?' Matt came back with in that horrible mocking drawl which she knew all too well. 'I've been the last word in discretion. It would be truer to say that I've covered up for you. I don't have to foul anything up for you, Tony. It seems to me that you're more than capable of doing that all by yourself.'

Then Tony responded, 'One lousy lapse. That's all it was. And you set me up for that. The pair of you used me to serve your own rotten ends. And I was stupid enough to fall.'

'In more ways than one. Don't be ridiculous, Tony. I'm quite certain that you didn't have to be dragged, and that you enjoyed . . . falling,' Matt returned.

Zoe didn't need Matt's tone to tell her that he wasn't referring to Tony's falling down the stairs; breaking a leg was no fun. She didn't wait to find out if Tony's lapse was going to be explained, though not to her credit, because it was wrong to eavesdrop on a private conversation; what made her move away was the approach of footsteps coming from the opposite direction. Hannah? She was going to feel very sneaky if Hannah caught her listening. So she squashed her curiosity and beat a hasty retreat back up to her own room, waiting there for a full five minutes before coming down again.

This time, to her intense relief, Hannah was also present. She smiled as she saw Zoe, the small, mystified frown on her forehead being quickly ironed out.

Had Hannah walked in while the argument was still in process, or was she puzzled because of the atmosphere that still prevailed? Matt's face was tight and coldly angry. Tony's was sullen, his mouth petulant. Big as they were, it wouldn't have surprised Zoe to see Hannah take hold of their heads and bang them together to drive some sense into them.

'What can I get you?' Matt barked out.

He wasn't looking at Zoe, he was staring at a point somewhere above her head, but as both Hannah and Tony had drinks, the inquiry could only have been directed at her.

'A small sherry, please,' she said.

Tony was sitting on the sofa, his crutches leaning against the arm. 'Sit here, darling,' he said, patting the place by his side.

His tone was so tender after Matt's brusqueness that she almost tripped over her own feet to get there. Tony's arm went straight round her shoulders, not in the casual way she was used to in front of others, but to draw her close up to his side. This move accomplished, his fingers drew caressing circles on her bare arm. Zoe's eyes flashed an urgent message at him to stop; such an open display had to be as embarrassing for Hannah as it was for her.

123

Hannah's smile never altered. She was doing her utmost to paper over the dissent by making light conversation. As well as being a self-confessed lover of the sound of her own voice, Hannah was also a great mediator, but not even her influence could bring things back to normal. Zoe greatly appreciated Hannah's loquacious tongue, which left her unable to get a word in. The tension had destroyed her own power of speech. It was a blessing that her 'yes' and 'no,' 'really,' and 'I agree,' sufficed. A break in Hannah's chatter didn't occur until Yvette came to announce that dinner was served, but she was certain that she observed relief on the older woman's chiseled features.

It was easier at the dinner table because everyone was occupied in eating. Zoe wasn't conscious of what she ate; it was undoubtedly superb, but it tasted like sawdust in her mouth. Even though Hannah was English, she ran her home on French lines, and the French were proud of the quality of their cuisine and revered their food. Eating was taken seriously; important as conversation was at a French table, it wasn't uncommon for it to be slotted into second place, so Zoe's staccato attempts to help Hannah out passed muster.

What exactly had Matt and Tony been quarreling over? The fact that Tony had told Matt that 'she' had chosen him, and that Matt was out of the running, must mean that the angry exchange had been over Zoe herself.

But what had Tony meant when he accused Matt of trying to foul it up for him? And what lapse was Tony guilty of?

At last the interminable meal, with its many courses, was over. Now just the ritual of taking coffee in the salon had to be observed. Hannah went ahead to alert Yvette to bring the tray in. Zoe scraped her chair back and went to retrieve Tony's crutches.

'Just bring one, darling. I can manage with that and your support.' As he gave the instruction Tony's eyes glided over to Matt.

Zoe didn't like the feeling that a contest was being waged. Or was she being unduly suspicious? Tony had been partaking heavily of the wine; perhaps he didn't feel capable of moving under his own steam. In any case, until she figured out what was going on, she decided that it was safer not to oppose him. She seemed to be in the middle of a combustible situation where the wrong move could detonate an ugly explosion.

She handed one crutch to Tony and stood helplessly by as he got to his feet and slid his arm possessively round her waist. Was Tony showing extra affection toward her because he thought she might be jealous at coming back and finding him with Camille? Was this his way of telling her that there was nothing in it and at the same time reaffirming his love for her? It would be nice to think it was something as simple as that. But it came too soon on the heels of her confession about knowing Matt for her liking. She couldn't help but wonder if Tony was gloating. Was this distasteful display designed to rub it in that she belonged to him? Whatever the reason, the walk into the salon was an act of ownership that made her blood boil.

Matt followed with the other crutch. She cast a swift backward glance and saw that he looked as if it wouldn't take much for him to hit Tony over the head with it.

When they reached the sofa she tried to free herself from Tony's hold, but his temporary disability hadn't robbed him of his strength and she was pulled down, the hand that accomplished this grazing her breast as it journeyed to secure her waist. She shot him a killing look, but she couldn't read a thing in his drink-glazed eyes. It was possible that he hadn't done it deliberately, she supposed.

She didn't know why, but it came to her most uncannily that the contest wasn't over her at all. She got the feeling that Tony was using her to score over Matt for something that had nothing to do with the present situation. Matt was a natural target for petty jealousy and grievances. But the people who begrudged him the position he'd carved out for himself were the kind she had no time for—the grumblers who wanted the wealth and the power but who weren't prepared to work hard to get it. Surely she couldn't suspect

Tony of being like that? She'd be thinking next that Tony had known of her old friendship with Matt from the very beginning and that he'd made a deliberate play for her to get back at Matt, which was crazy. There was no sense in that thought because Matt hadn't loved and lost her. He had dropped her. Tony wouldn't have been able to know that the old interest would be revived. In trying to reason things out, she was getting more and more muddled.

Hannah came into the room. Yvette followed her with the coffee tray, which she set down upon a table that was an exquisite period piece enriched with marquetry and ormolu mounts.

'Pour the coffee, please, Zoe,' Hannah requested.

Zoe hoped the relief she felt at the timely delivery from Tony's clutches wasn't evident in her expression. And if it was, she hoped that at least Hannah would realize that it was because she thought displays of affection, even between the most loving of engaged couples, should be kept for private moments.

Matt walked over to the liquor cabinet. 'Any takers?' he asked, glancing back.

Hannah considered. 'A small cointreau for me, I think, please.'

'Coming up! Zoe?'

'Nothing for me, thank you,' she said, looking up briefly from her task of pouring Hannah's coffee.

'Tony? I don't suppose you'll be declining,' Matt said.

Tony's jaw clenched. 'Cognac. A large one.'

Hannah reached out to take the delicate china cup from Zoe. 'Thank you, dear. Matt is fixing the car so that you'll be able to travel farther afield.'

'That's very kind of him,' Zoe responded pleasantly, even though she thought that getting the car on the road again was for Hannah's sake and not hers.

Hannah then said, 'You should take advantage of Matt while he's here and get him to take you around.'

'Zoe can take advantage of me any time she likes,' Matt inserted dryly.

Zoe had felt a distinct stirring of sympathy for Matt while Tony had been pawing her and gloating over his ownership of her. After that remark, she wondered why.

'Matt comes and goes with amazing speed,' Hannah chatted on regardless; 'so don't lose a moment's time, Zoe.'

'No, don't, Zoe.' Matt nodded in agreement.

'Do you want coffee, Matt?' Zoe asked, her eyes chilling him.

Not that he looked chilled as he replied, a faint smile touching his mouth, 'No, thank you. I'm going out.'

'That has the flavor of an assignation?' The inflexion in Hannah's tone turned the words

128

into a question.

'Monsieur Dupont is having a kind of old boys' reunion dinner. When I took Camille home earlier he asked me to join the party for a drink afterward . . .'

For the purpose of alleviating Camille's boredom, no doubt, Zoe thought.

'. . . no point in waiting up for me.'

'As if I would. I stopped waiting up for you years ago.' The puzzled look had returned to Hannah's face. Zoe could have told her the jibe was meant for her. 'Convey my fondest regards to André, and give Camille a kiss from me.'

'Will do.'

'I didn't think you would find that much hardship. And tell André that I want him and Camille to come over for dinner while you're still here. I'll get in touch with him very soon to arrange something.'

*   *   *

The next morning Zoe woke with the intention of avoiding a repeat of the previous day's breakfast encounter with Matt. Strategy was not required of her. A surreptitious peep along the balcony showed the remains of Matt's breakfast. He had eaten and apparently gone down.

Zoe made her way downstairs to find Hannah on the point of sitting down to breakfast on the terrace.

'Ah, Zoe! Good morning. I missed you yesterday. Were you earlier or later than me?'

Not only would a lie have been pointless, but if it was found out it would make it look as if she had something to hide. 'Neither. Matt was having breakfast on the balcony when I went out, and he asked me to join him.'

'That figures. Matt is one of the few men I know who's civil at breakfast time. Poor Tony is unbearable until he's read at least three pages of the morning newspaper and had two cups of coffee. He takes after his father, my late son-in-law, in that.'

'Tony, presumably, isn't up yet?'

'I don't think Tony will be putting in an appearance for some time. He had too much to drink last night.'

'I noticed.'

'He'll be sleeping it off. He doesn't say a lot, and I'm not saying that I approve of excess drinking, but I think he's in considerable pain with his leg. He doesn't seem as mobile as he should be. Do be tolerant of him.'

Zoe thought that Tony's lack of mobility came from laziness. It couldn't have been easy to adjust, and she did sympathize with him, but she found his lack of effort something to deplore. As for Tony's 'not saying a lot,' Hannah must have been wearing ear muffs; he was forever complaining about how much discomfort he was in. However, Zoe felt that she'd received one gentle rebuke for her dry agreement on Tony's drunken state, so she smiled and promised, 'I'll try.'

'Good girl. I knew you would. Something's going on between Matt and Tony, although I don't know what.' The shrewd eyes looked appraisingly at Zoe for a moment. When nothing was forthcoming, Hannah continued, 'It's laughable really, but Tony is nearer Matt's age than Matt is to Tony's mother, his own sister. Because of that they've always been more like brothers than uncle and nephew. Even if there's no cause, brothers will always make up something to fight about. Perhaps I was too old when I had Matt. It shames me to say it, but I've never properly understood him. He was as naughty as any small boy . . . but the way he always accepted the blame, no, that wasn't natural.'

'You're saying that as if you don't think that accepting the blame is a good trait. Surely it's better than trying to wriggle out of it?'

'I agree, but sometimes Matt was punished when the punishment wasn't justified. He would never explain why he'd acted in the particular way he had. The reason for doing something sometimes cancels out the wrong. I could never get that across to Matt. If he'd done something, he'd done it, and there was no place for ifs and whys in his reasoning. The action always had to stand up on its own. He has this stubborn streak in him that doesn't

131

allow for mitigating circumstances or acknowledge weakness in any form. If he's intolerant of others—and I must admit that I sometimes think he's too hard on Tony—then he's equally hard on himself. He's not had things easy. There's a part of his life that he's sensitive about. There was this girl . . .' Hannah broke off in some confusion. 'You're such an easy person to talk to, Zoe. And perhaps I would find it a relief to talk about it to someone sympathetic. But Matt's hurt is his own affair, and to talk about it would be a betrayal of him. So not another word.'

Even though her curiosity was fully aroused, Zoe knew that it wasn't fair to probe. With a faint sigh of regret she switched to something else, something she felt needed to be said. 'I owe you an apology, Hannah.'

'An apology? Whatever for?'

'For any indelicacy you may have observed yesterday. Tony was very affectionate.'

'Yes, he was.'

Hannah's steady regard of her told Zoe that this wasn't going her way at all.

'I thought . . . I was afraid you might think it would have been better if . . . if he'd waited until we were alone.' It had been quite painful to stammer out that admission. Need Hannah look so amused?

'Oh, Zoe, I may be old, but not that old! That was the first healthy sign I've seen between you. Since you've been here, the pair

132

of you have been acting as though the fire had gone out of your feelings. My dear late husband and I were more than man and wife, we had a passionate affair until the day he died. Of course, he was twenty years my senior, so I knew that if nature followed its course he would go first. That being so, we were never complacent about one another. We made the most of every moment we had together, sometimes at the expense of others. Matt suffered more than Nerissa. With him arriving on the scene fifteen years after she did, his father was more like his grandfather. The time we had together was slipping away and doubly precious, but that was no excuse, and looking back I realize that we were selfish to shut Matt out. Then, when my husband died, I withdrew into myself. I condemn Matt for being intolerant of weakness, in himself as well as others, but I'm to blame for that. I let him get on with growing up all by himself, and on the whole he's made an excellent job of it. I'm a very lucky woman that we're so close now. It would have been easy for him to bear a grudge for my shortcomings. But then, he's his father's son, with his father's strong character.'

'I think there's one trait that Matt gets from you. You're being too hard on yourself. You're not allowing for the mitigating circumstances.'

'Thank you, Zoe. That's very kind of you.'

'It must have been wonderful to know a love like yours.'

133

'It was, even if it was sometimes a strain. Things were more formal in those days, attitudes more correct. It was difficult to conform and not flaunt our feelings. We were like young lovers to the end. We couldn't bear to be out of one anther's sight. But why should this surprise you, Zoe?'

'It wasn't like that with my parents. They loved one another dearly, I'm sure of that, but not in the way you describe. My mother once tried to explain it to me. She said that their love was constant, like the moon. She said it was better to have a lasting love like that than a love that had all the passion and fire of a meteorite, but would eventually burn itself out.'

'It isn't a foregone conclusion that one love will end any quicker than the other. And even if the danger was there, I would always go for the passion and the fire. Perhaps what your mother had was right for her. I would be the last to suggest otherwise or question her judgment. But it wouldn't have been right for me, and I know it wouldn't be right for you. You might put on a cool façade, but at heart you're a deeply passionate woman. Don't go against your nature, child. At your age it wouldn't be right. At my time of life it's possible to settle for second best, *perhaps* . . . I'm going to tell you something in the strictest confidence. My dear friend, André Dupont, has asked me to marry him several times. I'm not really sure of my reasons for saying no. I'm not looking for another meteorite, not at my age. Anyway, who knows but that it's in the stars that we're only capable of one all-consuming love.'

Zoe left Hannah to her thoughts, her memories, touched by the confidences she had been entrusted with, but not totally convinced. The beliefs of a lifetime couldn't be torn down in moments, and Zoe had too high a regard for her mother's wisdom to doubt those long-ago words said to the impressionable child she had been. But she thought about the things Hannah had said, on and off, all day. Most of her concentration went to the incident concerning Matt and the girl. A part of his life Matt was sensitive about, Hannah had said. Had this girl turned him down and left him antimarriage? Had she hurt him very much, and was that why he was the way he was now? Was that why he used women and wouldn't let any one woman come too close to him? Perhaps something in him had been destroyed by his lonely childhood and this later traumatic event, and he was incapable of acting differently. But surely all this proved that her mother's beliefs were right? Matt's meteoric affair with the girl had burned itself out, on her side at least, leaving Matt hurt and cynical.

*   *   *

She had done her duty, sitting with Tony for much of the day, sympathizing with him for feeling off color, even though she knew he was merely suffering the effects of a hangover. But finally she'd had enough of trying to amuse him and decided to stretch her legs before getting ready for dinner.

She was halfway down the road when she heard the healthy purr of a car engine. All she'd seen all day of Matt was two legs sticking out from under Hannah's car. Now his jubilant face smiled at her from behind the windshield. He pulled up alongside her and poked his head out the open window.

'Success?' she said.

He gave an affirmative nod. 'Sure thing.'

She noticed that he'd changed out of his oil-stained jeans into casual slacks and a cool-looking gray and blue shirt, its open neck showing his deeply tanned throat. His attractiveness constricted her own throat, and she wondered if he was on his way to see Camille again.

It took her by surprise when he cocked his chin at a jaunty angle and said, 'I'm doing a test drive. Fancy coming with me?'

Didn't she just! The temptation was irresistible. She asked herself what harm Matt could get up to in the short time before they had to return so they could get ready for the evening meal. She was wearing separates, a jazzy mint-green suntop and a lemon cotton skirt with patch pockets and a wide waistband to show off her trim waist. Neither of them was suitably dressed to sit at Hannah's table.

With a small reckless laugh she said, 'Why not?'

The passenger door was opened for her and she got in.

It was a beautiful day ready to slide into a beautiful evening, and some small renegade part of her wished they didn't have to return in a hurry. She wished that Matt was taking her for a long drive with a leisurely meal at the end of it. Somewhere quiet and intimate where they could begin again, get to know one another afresh. The breeze from the open window whipped her hair across her face. As she removed it from her mouth she contemplated her madness at letting such a thought into her head.

CHAPTER SEVEN

She should have been concentrating on the passing scenery, but her gaze kept being dragged back to the clean-cut obduracy of his profile, the competence of his hands on the wheel, the tantalizing strength of his thigh.

'Where are we going?' she asked.

'No particular destination. Just following my nose. Why?'

'Don't go too far. Remember Hannah's predilection for punctuality.'

'Can one go too far, Zoe?'

The sensual intonation was deliberate.

'Stop that, Matt.'

'Stop what? I haven't touched you.'

'Just see that you don't.'

'If you say so. I'm law-abiding at heart. I obey the rules of society and adhere strictly to the highway code, or any code. If you put up prohibitive signs, I'll observe them.'

She believed him, so why did she feel uneasy? Determinedly she turned and made herself look out the car window, but although she pretended to be totally absorbed, she was too conscious of Matt to banish him wholly from her thoughts.

They were traveling in an easterly direction, following what was supposed to be one of the most picturesque roads in Europe. For a while the car hugged the coastline of the Côte d'Azur, named for its blue and sparkling sea. The area was sheltered by the Alps, and its exceptionally mild climate produced vegetation like that in much hotter countries, palms, dates, oranges, bananas, and pomegranates. And flowers, everywhere flowers. Then Matt pointed the nose of the car inland, and they climbed a secondary road through magnificent mountain scenery with beautiful views of the sea below.

'Next time you're dabbing scent behind your

ears, bear in mind that the rose, violet, hyacinth, or whatever it was made from was probably grown not too far from here.'

'Is that a fact?' Zoe said, although it was something she had already read somewhere and stored away. The area was noted for the large amount of flowers it grew for sale in London and Paris and for making perfume.

Never again would she take out a perfume stopper without thinking of that moment. Yet no bottled fragrance could equal the scent carried on the warm breeze.

'I've got a feeling we're going to be late getting back,' Zoe despaired, the words a contradiction to her deep sigh of content.

'Does it matter?'

'I shall stand behind you and let you take the brunt of Hannah's wrath.'

'What about your fiancé's wrath?'

Why did he have to remind her of Tony? 'His, too,' she said.

'Coward.'

'Perhaps I just like a quiet life.' She didn't care if he did read a double meaning into that. Life with Tony would be more tranquil than with him. 'I think we should turn back now. But first, can we stop, please, and get out to look at the view?'

'Of course.'

He slowed and pulled in at the first convenient place.

As she got out of the car he said, 'Does it

constitute touching you if I hold your hand? Not because I want to hold your hand, of course, but because it's the gentlemanly thing to do to help a lady over rough ground.'

His mood was too mischievous. She didn't trust it. But she gave him her hand as they walked to what Matt assured her would be the best vantage point. When they stopped, Zoe drew her breath in sharply. It seemed unfair that this sun-drenched corner of the earth should abound with so much beauty. It was a miracle of nature that no mortal painter, no matter how delicate his touch, could reproduce. The last rays of the sun brushed deep shafts of coppery gold over the earth, animating each rock and tree, every sweeping line and plane of color, down to the sparkling, breathtaking blue of the sea.

Zoe's eyes soaked it all up. She was still savoring it in wonder and awe when she felt the first soft suspicion of a raindrop. She looked up at the sky. Surely its loss of vivid blue was because of the fading daylight? It was incomprehensible that rain would spoil this lovely day, and she dismissed the feather touch on her cheek as imagination, until it was joined by another . . . and another. The gentle cascade gained momentum and grew into a shower which, with relentless, fiendish speed, turned into a drenching downpour. Matt took her hand and they ran back toward the car. The rain beat them back with tropical force.

They plowed on, feet squelching, blindly scurrying for the cover of the car. What had initially seemed a short walk was a waterlogged nightmare on the return trip.

Matt wrenched open the door for her, his hands closing on her hips and pushing her in before he ran round to the other side and got in himself.

Grinning across at her, he said, 'Why do you look wetter than I do?'

'Possibly because I am wetter than you are. Long hair,' she explained tersely, opening the car door for a brief moment, making a rope of her offending tresses, and wringing out the excess water.

She couldn't have been more sodden if she'd swum underwater to get back. Despite her efforts, her hair was still streaming. Her skirt adhered to her thighs, and she dreaded to think what the tightly clinging suntop was revealing, although it was doubtful if it was anything he hadn't already guessed from the low cut of the back.

'You'd probably do better to take that off and lay it out on the back seat to dry,' he said, giving one slender strap a tweak.

'Probably,' she said, 'but you know I'm not going to—and why.'

'I'd see as much any day if I walked on a beach at St. Tropez,' he said, but he didn't press the issue. He extracted a clean, folded handkerchief, which was miraculously dry, from his pocket. 'Not much, I'm afraid,' he said, gently patting her face, 'but the best I can do.'

'I'll survive until we get back. Why are you just sitting there, Matt? Why don't you start the engine and get moving?'

'Slight problem. Well, actually, major problem. Did you notice the poor condition of the road we've just traveled up, not to mention its steepness?'

'Yes, but you're competent. You're more than just an average driver.'

'In normal circumstances. These aren't normal circumstances.'

'I'm not afraid. I'd rather get back than stay here while it abates. I'll feel perfectly safe with you.'

'Don't bet on that. I might risk my neck, but I'm not risking yours.'

'Would you stop procrastinating and kindly explain what you mean?'

'The windshield wipers don't work. I was going to fix them tomorrow.'

'I don't believe you. You're making it up.'

He switched on the engine and fiddled about on the dashboard. Nothing happened.

'I do believe you!' she gasped.

'I'm sorry, Zoe. I didn't know it was going to rain.'

'I know you didn't.' But she also knew he wasn't sorry.

Something was knocking at her brain, some

gleam of intelligent reasoning that demanded to be admitted. The triumphant look on Matt's face was akin to the one that had been on Tony's face the previous evening at dinner when he'd pawed and fondled her just to make Matt squirm. Matt had asked her to come out on a drive with him to get even. He had never intended to get her back to Les Charmettes in time for dinner; perhaps he meant to keep her out all night!

Oh, he hadn't arranged the rain, but it had been a godsend. When it had started raging down like that, she bet, he undoubtedly couldn't believe his luck. It had saved him from having to engineer some excuse for not being able to take her back, the most likely one being the old classic of the car failing its after-repair test drive. It would have broken down at the crucial moment, possibly when it was too dark for him to find out what the trouble was, and so they would have had to stay put until morning.

Not because he wanted to spend the night with her. That was the choking, humiliating part, but to score off Tony. She'd had the feeling the night before that she was being used to settle a difference. What had been an idle thought then grew into a certainty now. Neither Matt nor Tony really cared about her, except as a weapon to use against each other.

Her fury knew no bounds. She dragged open the car door, but before she could get

143

out Matt's steel fingers wrapped round her arm.

'Where do you think you're going?'

'Anywhere to get away from you. I remember passing a village a little way back. I'll head for it. I won't stay here with you.'

'It's pouring. You'll get washed away.'

'I can't feel a bigger drip than I already do for falling for this rotten setup.'

'What are you talking about?'

'You never meant to get me back in time for dinner. I doubt if you meant to get me back tonight. Can you deny it?'

'Why should I? You can think what you damn well like; but you're not getting out of this car. The village you're talking about is too far away for you to walk it in this. There's a better prospect a few kilometers ahead.'

He switched on the ignition again; the engine hummed to life, and he wound his window right down and put the car headlights on at full beam.

'What are you doing?'

'What does it look as if I'm doing? I'm taking you there, aren't I?'

'This is crazy,' she said as he swung the car back onto the road.

'Not half as crazy as letting you walk.'

He drove with his head stuck out the window, and she wished that she hadn't flown off the handle. She wondered what her stupidity had let them in for.

144

'Don't be afraid,' he yelled at her. 'I've been in worse than this. You should have seen some of the walls of fog I've driven through. I've got a built-in radar system that I switch on at times like these.'

But even trusting him more than she would have trusted any other man, she was still afraid. A sheet of rain battered at his face. 'Pull in somewhere, Matt. This is madness.' But either he didn't hear, or he didn't want to hear, because he kept on relentlessly. In the end she held her breath, and it seemed to her that she didn't let it out again until his target was reached. A building of some sort swam mistily into view. He pulled into a yard and didn't look at her until he'd shut off the engine and wound the window back up.

'You could have killed us both,' she accused, her relief at being safe exploding into anger.

He took her face in his hands. The tenderness of the action melted her anger away. 'No, I couldn't, Zoe. I knew what I was doing. I might take the odd calculated risk, but I never take foolhardy ones. What do you want most in the world at this moment?'

The rain had been beating in at them through the open car window and Zoe was soaked again, 'To feel dry,' she said.

'And to sit down and eat a civilized meal?' he inquired.

'That would be a bonus.'

But first another bonus was coming her way.

She knew it, but she didn't seem able to draw back from it. A profound sense of unreality gripped her as his hands gathered her close, molding themselves to her wet, clinging suntop, finding the sweetness of her breast and sending tingling sensations through her body. A wildness sang in her blood as his mouth sought and devoured hers. He hadn't broken his word not to touch her. 'If you put up prohibitive signs, I'll observe them,' was what he'd promised. She hadn't. All barriers were down.

It was madness. Divine madness. Her fingers obeyed impulses that she had previously managed to resist, wriggling open a button of his shirt and sliding inside to press themselves against the hard wall of his chest, and then, appeasing an intolerable curiosity, they tangled in the masculine growth of hair. Even damp, it was slightly wiry to the touch, a sensuous experience.

She felt a shiver run through him. Her other hand went up in time to follow a ripple moving along his throat. In that strange moment it was as if they had reversed roles, as if she was the one using him for sexual pleasure and he was the vulnerable partner. He was back in control with shattering quickness, her moment of power lost as he reseized the advantage she had stolen. He was on top again, the supreme male dominating her into bliss as he kissed the hollow at the base of her throat. His fingers moved to her shoulders, bringing down the straps of her suntop and then playing along her naked back, sending tingles down her spine, coming round to entrance her breasts with a light touch that enchanted and delighted her. The velvet caresses of his fingertips hardened her nipples; then his lips softly brushed them each in turn before lifting to tease her temple.

In the ensuing moment the nature of the sensuous game he was playing came to her. He hadn't lost the upper hand, not for one single moment. She hadn't seduced his senses when she touched him. The seducer was playing a subtle trick on her. She hadn't stolen the initiative just then, he had given it to her. And he was giving it to her again, but, if he'd done his inveigling well, this time she would make a bolder foray. And so it would go on. He would dominate, and then appear to be dominated, instilling in her a false sense of security by letting her think that she was on top of the situation and could call a halt at any time she chose. But the controlling power had never left his hands. He had banked on her not being aware of that until she'd advanced to the point of no return, when both she and their joint passions were totally out of anyone's control.

In the heady moment of realization, her senses on fire, her desire stoked to an impossible high by his superb cunning and mastery, she didn't know how to handle the situation; she didn't even know if she *could* handle it.

When he brought the straps of her suntop back up over her shoulders, her sluggish brain couldn't make sense of the action. It took several seconds for it to sink in that sitting in a car in someone else's yard provided neither the comfort nor the privacy for what he had in mind.

'I'm glad you attempted to make that crazy break,' he said thickly. 'I had this place half in mind. I'm glad you forced the issue. If we've got to wait the storm out, why not do it in comfort?'

'Why not?' she echoed in an oddly strangled voice.

'But I didn't know how you'd take the idea—the idea of driving through the rain to get here, that is.'

'I wouldn't have been wildly enthusiastic. What is this place, by the way?'

'It used to be a farmhouse, but it's been converted into a *logis*. In case you don't know, a *logis* is a small, modest hotel. But don't let that fool you. I'd give this one the four-star rating of a first-class establishment. The patron and his wife, Jean-Claude and Berthe Poussin, have a name for keeping a good table and an impressive wine cellar. I've eaten here myself, so I know it's true. I've never had occasion to need overnight accommodation, but I've heard that the rooms, although simple,

148

are clean and comfortable. Not that we're likely to need them. By the time we've eaten the rain is certain to have stopped, but you never know.'

Mellowed with good food and free-flowing wine, you never knew; that was what he meant. He might not know, but she did. She was on her mettle now and she had no intention of being manipulated by his playful feather caresses and led into indiscretion by his oh-so-innocent and oh-so-lethal charm.

Madame Poussin gave them an effusive welcome. Zoe didn't understand a word the woman said, but 'clucking' was the same in any language. Matt translated for her. 'Madame didn't expect anyone to come on such a night. She is distressed at the thought of letting you sit down to eat in those wet clothes, and she would be delighted to loan you something to wear while she takes your things through to the kitchen to dry.'

Madame Poussin was considerably shorter than Zoe and very plump. She was as round as a butter-ball. Thinking of herself in Madame's clothes made Zoe want to laugh. It was an effort to keep her mouth straight as she answered Matt. 'Please tell Madame that I'm very grateful, and that it's a kind offer, but I won't trouble her. I'll soon dry out.'

This was duly relayed to Madame Poussin, who threw up her hands as another unintelligible spate of words issued from her mouth.

Matt again turned to face Zoe, conspiratorial laughter in his eyes—although when she came to think about it, perhaps he wasn't laughing with her but at her. 'Madame says it's no trouble, and that you will be more comfortable and her mind will be happier if you will permit her to fix you out, or words to that effect. I think you'd better go with her, Zoe. Otherwise I don't think there's much hope of our being fed.'

'What about you? What about your wet clothes?' He shrugged. 'No mention about that. Perhaps I'm supposed to be made of hardier stuff. That, or I shall suddenly be besieged to follow some equally insistent male.'

'I hope so.' *I hope Monsieur Poussin turns out to be a roly-poly midget and you look every bit as stupid as I'm going to look.* Her eyes flashed this message to him; then she put on a brave smile, nodded her acceptance, and allowed Madame to conduct her to an upstairs room.

A wardrobe door was swung open, and although Zoe didn't understand the verbal instructions, the accompanying gestures encouraged her to choose something.

Still Zoe hesitated, not wanting to select Madame's best apparel. With an understanding grin, Madame decided to make the selection herself and took out an exceptionally pretty dress with a tiny green and blue star pattern on a white background. It was, if Zoe was any judge, exactly her size. Madame then beckoned for Zoe to follow her and this time led the way into a bathroom, pointed to the large fluffy towel on the towel rack, and left Zoe to get on with it.

When Zoe joined Matt again she felt clean and tidy, her hair restored to its former bounce and silky texture.

His eyes flicked over her with approval. 'Madame was right. Her daughter must be about your size. Anne-Marie's dress could have been made for you.'

'You rotter. You could have told me.'

'You're too quick at jumping to conclusions, Zoe. That should serve as a lesson,' he said, taking her elbow and guiding her into the dining room.

It had a subdued, cozy intimacy, with the candles and soft lighting throwing a warm rosy glow everywhere. Red tablecloths were on the tables and snowy white napkins had been folded to resemble water lilies.

Only two other tables were taken, giving the tiny dining room an almost spacious look. It would have appeared to be bursting at the seams if it had been fully occupied. A corner table was set for them.

'I ordered for you. Is that all right?'

Zoe sank comfortably into a deep wall-seat upholstered in dark red velvet, relaxing amid

151

the eye-pleasing decor and the luxury of feeling dry and deliciously pampered. 'Yes, lovely.'

'The womenfolk wait on the tables, Madame and her daughter, Anne-Marie.'

At that precise moment Madame appeared. A bottle was presented for Matt's inspection. He gave an affirmative nod, and pale golden liquid flowed into tall, thin-stemmed glasses.

Zoe raised her glass to her lips, savoring the bouquet with her nose before satisfying her palate.

Madame departed and Matt resumed speaking. 'Jean-Claude is the chef. He takes his art seriously. He creates each course, rather than prepares it. It could be a—'

'Gastronomic treat,' Zoe said as a trolley of hors d'oeuvres was wheeled alongside the table by a young French girl.

Zoe's mouth moistened at the sight of all the silver dishes, each arranged so that the artistic assortments of delectable, and delectably colored, foods tempted the eye as it invited the juices to flow. There were crisp celery curls; tomatoes filled with white bread-crumbs, garlic, and herbs; stuffed eggs and thumb-sized artichokes; sardines; mussels in a marinade; tiny pink shrimps in lemon juice; thin slices of sausage and ham; tiny French beans; and black olives glistening in a dressing of oil and herbs.

The French girl heaped Zoe's plate and set

it before her. Zoe asked Matt if this was Anne-Marie. On being told that it was, Zoe then asked Matt to thank her for the loan of the dress. This done, Matt faced Zoe and relayed Anne-Marie's reply. 'She says it's her pleasure. She also says that she didn't realize how pretty the dress was, but perhaps it looks that way because you are so much prettier than she is.'

'Thank Anne-Marie, but tell her that's not so. She's much prettier than I am.'

'I will, but with tongue in cheek. Either you're very modest, Zoe, or you don't look in your mirror often enough.' Anne-Marie walked away moments later, her lips turned up in pleasure at Matt's words. 'Before Anne-Marie arrived, you interrupted too quickly. I hope it will be a gastronomic treat. But what I was going to say was that it could be a lengthy business. While you were upstairs putting on Anne-Marie's lovely dress I phoned Les Charmettes and spoke to my mother. I explained our predicament.'

'I'm glad you thought of that and managed to get through. I wouldn't like Hannah to be worried.'

'She wasn't. You, I, and the car were missing. She did some simple arithmetic and came up with the right answer. She knew that you would be safe with me.'

'And Tony?'

'Ah, now, that's a different matter entirely. Mother said that he's been most agitated and so she would be happy to put his mind at rest.'

The horrible mocking grin was back on Matt's mouth. Far from being at rest, Tony's mind would be even more agitated, wondering what was happening and what they were up to, and Matt was reveling in that knowledge. Tony knew that she was still attracted to Matt, and he didn't trust Matt any more than she did.

'Everything satisfactory?' Matt inquired, his voice as bland and as smooth as the mayonnaise coating the eggs.

It was another of his remarks with a double meaning. She answered as if she had recognized only the innocent one. In the best French tradition, the vegetables were either raw or almost raw. She crunched on a bean. 'Entirely.' Her tone was as sharp as the well-seasoned vinaigrette dressing the bean had been dipped in.

Anne-Marie returned to whisk away the plates. The first course had done its trick, awakening but not satisfying, rousing and exciting tastebuds for what was to come: bass grilled with fennel, which was a speciality of the region. That was followed by duck with grapes and wine sauce. Matt hadn't ordered dessert ahead. He chose French apple pie, distinguished from the English version by a top 'crust' made of sliced apple instead of pastry. Zoe asked for the tiniest portion, a mere token taste, of a light as whipped cream *bavaroise* dashed with Grand Marnier. Her wineglass had been refilled during the meal, and she declined the brandy Matt tried to press on her with her coffee.

Zoe enjoyed the fragrance coming from the enormous iridescent glass that Matt lifted to his lips in an abstract and wholly contented way. He had sat across from her during the meal, but now he joined her on the cushioned wall-seat. The gentle lighting, the shimmering glow of the candles, softened the hard planes of his face. It seemed impossible to believe him capable of a devious or culpable act, yet evidence that he was came from the strong fingers that encircled her wrist and drew patterns in the palm of her hand in a disturbingly intimate way. The pressure of his hard thigh against hers increased her feeling of excitement.

The brandy swirled as he offered her a sip from his glass. It was no accident that her lips were directed to the spot where his hand touched. The brandy exploded with an aromatic warmth in her mouth and throat; her lips tingled as though at his kiss. He lifted the glass to his own mouth, covering the exact same spot. His eyes caressed her over the brim, and again her lips burned as if he'd kissed them.

It was getting near decision time, and Zoe knew it, but she didn't seem capable of lucid thought. Seduced by the good food and wine and Matt's sumptuous attentiveness, she wanted to float forever on this euphoric cloud of content. The rest of her body wanted its share of the shivery things he was doing to her hand under the discreet cover of the tablecloth. Feeling that she was under the influence of some mesmeric pull, she snatched her fingers away. His eyes mocked her as his fingers concentrated their wicked attention elsewhere, subjecting her thigh to the sensual torment.

She hadn't noticed that the dining room had filled up until Matt drew her attention to the fact. 'More refugees from the rain, do you suppose?'

'It could have stopped raining,' she said.

'Exactly what I was afraid of.'

The illusion of privacy had already been dispelled, so it was no intrusion when Madame Poussin came to their table to present the bill and ask if they had enjoyed their meal. Matt translated her words for Zoe, who asked, 'Will you add something extra for the loan of the dress?'

'I already have,' he said, tucking a quantity of francs into the folded slip of paper.

Zoe beamed a smile at Madame, which was returned in full measure. More conversation passed between Madame and Matt, during which time a wry little smile touched Matt's mouth, setting Zoe's curiosity alight.

Her eyes followed Madame's disappearing back. 'What was that about?'

'Your clothes are dry and in the upstairs room where Madame escorted you earlier. She said for you to make your way up there and change back when you're ready.'

'That wasn't all she said.'

'No.' Laughter gleamed from beneath his half-lowered lids.

'Aren't you going to tell me? You delight in teasing me, don't you?'

'You're so delightful to tease. Perhaps, if you're a very good girl, I'll tell you later.'

She knew that she would get no more out of him for now. 'I'll go change out of my borrowed finery,' she decided.

Upstairs again, she took off Anne-Marie's dress and hung it on the outside of the wardrobe for Madame to find. In her own simple suntop and skirt she went back downstairs to where Matt was waiting for her. Madame and Anne-Marie came to say goodbye, and in this they were joined by Monsieur Poussin. Matt took her hand as they walked out.

It was a beautiful night, the stars burning vividly in the sky. It was impossible to believe it had rained so heavily, except for the fact that the air was even more redolent of flowers, the way it always was after a storm.

The drive back to Les Charmettes was companionably silent. Matt parked the car in the drive. It was a natural place to park, but it was also out of sight of the house.

157

Zoe's instincts didn't have to be all that alert for her to know that she should make a run for it. She would have, too, but for the detaining hand that came out to clamp round her wrist. Her lips tingled as they had earlier in anticipation of the real thing. The promise of his kiss hovered in the air between them as his fingers moved up her arm, sending dangerous flames of passion through her veins. His mouth came so gently to hers that, although the kiss was expected, the fiery explosion it set off took her by surprise. It was like a fever attacking her brain and weakening her pulse, reducing her resistance to a whimper that escaped her lips before the delicious onslaught began again.

The heat burned her up and melted her bones. His hands filled themselves with her breasts, before wandering up and over her shoulders, down her spine, molding her to him, closing round her hips. Then his voice was rasping against her forehead, vibrating with impatience. 'This damned car is too restrictive. Why aren't we in bed together, Zoe? We could have been. We still could be.'

She tried to form the word 'no,' but it wouldn't come.

'I'm human, Zoe. I'm tired of just making it so far. I want all the joy.' His voice cracked. 'That's ironic.'

'What is?' she managed hoarsely.

'It's too near the bone to what Madame

said.'

'After that, you're going to have to tell me.'

'I suppose I am. Madame said she knew we were going to be very happy together, and that you would give me a lot of joy.'

'She said that?' The way Matt said it made it seem coarse, and Madame Poussin was the epitome of sweetness and refinement. Then it clicked. 'Madame saw my engagement ring and thought that you and I . . . ?

'Yes.'

Suddenly Zoe was angry, angrier than she could ever remember being in her life. 'How very quaint of Madame. You can get all the joy you want without marriage—but not from me. I admit that I almost lost my head for a while, but I'm on an even keel now. I've been here before. I was nineteen and ready to give everything. And almost did. No man had ever touched me in that way before. You said you'd come back. When you didn't I died a thousand times of humiliation. It won't happen again.'

'It wouldn't, Zoe, I can explain.'

'You're five years too late. I'll explain it to you. You didn't want me until I belonged to Tony. And now you only want me to get me away from him. I'm not giving you that satisfaction.'

'The hell you aren't!'

'You're a poor loser, Matt. Can't you get it through your head that you've lost?'

With that she opened the car door and ran

159

into the darkened house. She didn't stop running until she was in her own room with the door closed and locked behind her.

CHAPTER EIGHT

She didn't like asking, and perhaps it wouldn't get her anywhere at all, but she had to try.

'Tony, what is it between you and Matt?' It was more firmly implanted in her mind than ever that Matt had intended to keep her out the night before to get even with Tony.

'What do you mean?'

Tony was pretending not to know what she was getting at, but he looked uneasy.

'I'm referring to this constant struggle for one-upmanship. I know you're not going to like my saying this, and I apologize in advance, but sometimes I get the feeling that you're jealous of Matt.'

He said sulkily, 'If I am, I've every right to be. I'd be his partner, instead of being just another name on the payroll, if he hadn't cheated my father.'

It was so preposterous that she almost laughed out loud. 'Matt cheated your father!' Her hostility didn't blind her to the fact that Matt wouldn't cheat anyone.

'It started off as a partnership.'

'Yes, I remember that. Hunter & Talbot.

160

I've wondered about the Talbot.'

'That was my father. The business was going through a rocky period, and Matt used the famous persuasive Hunter charm to buy my father out. With his luck, straight away things started to pick up, and look how big he's coining it in now. I shouldn't be working for a paycheck. By rights I should be getting an equal share of the proceeds.'

Zoe frowned. She knew all about the persuasive Hunter charm. She was a strong character, but it had got to her on several occasions. She reviewed her opinion because of this. Could there be an element of truth in Tony's claim? She recalled what Matt had said when the question of Tony's working for him had cropped up once. 'I fulfill my obligation by employing him,' had been the words he'd used. She had thought that the word 'obligation' was a strange choice at the time. And she knew there was no love lost between Nerissa, Tony's mother, and Matt. Was the grudge because he had cheated her late husband?

It wasn't an easy day. Zoe spent it avoiding Matt and making amends to Tony for not returning in time for dinner the previous evening, staying by his side and giving him her full attention. Tony mellowed under her pampering, and the situation more or less returned to the way it had been.

The next morning the breakfast things hadn't had time to be cleared from the table on the terrace where Hannah, Tony, and Zoe still lingered over coffee when Camille put in an appearance.

She was wearing red again—and why not? The color which Zoe was never quite happy in because it clashed with her hair was the perfect foil for Camille's exotic coloring, her olive skin and ebony hair that had a sheen of silky blueness in the play of morning sunlight.

Zoe still didn't feel at ease with the younger girl, who was accepted at Les Charmettes as one of the family. Camille's smile was pleasant enough on the surface, but there was an underlying antagonism which, Zoe realized not without a little shame, was reciprocated.

The moment Matt sauntered up to join them, Camille's dainty hand slid into the crook of his arm in a proprietary way while at the same time she darted an outrageously flirtatious glance at Tony.

Matt's manner toward Camille was one of indulgence. She amused him, and he might not be averse to her carrying that amusement a stage further, if it hadn't progressed to that already. A swift inspection of her fiancé's face revealed to Zoe that Tony also found Camille's luscious curves very easy on the eye.

Camille looked cajolingly up at Matt. '*Chéri*, as I was having breakfast, I thought how nice it would be to spend the day in the company of an entertaining and handsome man, and you immediately came to mind.'

'Camille, how would you like to come out with me for the day?' he obliged amiably.

'Why, Matt,' she said, fluttering her eyelashes in an absurd parody of surprise. 'How kind of you to ask me. I'd love to.'

'What a delightfully incorrigible child,' Hannah observed fondly.

'Oh, delightfully,' Zoe said, the acid in her tone almost burning her lips.

Zoe was too busy trying to take herself in hand to notice the narrowing of Hannah's glance as she suggested, 'Why don't you young people make up a foursome?'

'Zoe?' Matt queried, looking directly into her eyes, a contact she had managed to avoid since being caught in the rain with him.

She shrugged to convey indifference. 'Why not?' The truth was, a day out would be a pleasant diversion. Even though Matt represented all the danger of a raging fire, she couldn't get burned with Tony and Camille there, 'If Tony feels up to it,' she qualified.

'It will be wonderful to get my rear onto a car seat. I feel as though it's been permanently glued to a lounger.'

'That's your fault,' Hannah said, with more than a little asperity in her tone. 'Nobody's expecting you to run a marathon, but . . .'

'I couldn't run if someone offered me a million.'

'No. But you could get about more than you have if you made the effort.'

Zoe had tried that one herself to rouse Tony from his apathy, but all she'd got in return was, 'You don't know what it's like.' Hannah didn't get that in so many words, but his look said as much.

*   *   *

Camille sat in the front of the car with Matt. Zoe squeezed into a corner of the back; because of his leg Tony took up most of the rear seat. They hadn't discussed where to go and they were already mobile when Matt said, 'Any preference?'

That was difficult. Obviously Tony wasn't up to doing a lot of walking. Camille was the first to answer. Giggling, she said, 'How do you fancy swapping one lounger for another, Tony?'

'Fine by me. Where did you have it in mind for this lounger to be positioned?' Tony asked.

'St. Trop.'

'That will definitely score on the view from Nan's garden,' was Tony's laughing reply.

'I've been known to be part of that view,' Camille said, pouting at him.

'You'll still be part of my view, won't you?' Tony quipped back. 'Perhaps more so.'

Zoe missed the implication of that in her consternation at not having had the common sense to equip herself with a swimsuit underneath her sundress.

164

'Does St. Tropez meet with your approval, Zoe?' Matt asked.

'Apart from the fact that I'm not wearing a swimsuit, yes. I didn't think.'

'No problem. St. Tropez is famous for a lot of things, including its fashionable shops. We can buy whatever we need. Swimwear, beach towels, tanning lotion.'

They went by way of the pretty coastal road with beautiful views of the sea. As they approached St. Tropez the buildup of traffic reduced their speed to a crawl.

'I think it would be best to drop Tony and Camille off, to save Tony the exertion of unnecessary walking. You, of course, will come with me, Zoe. I'll find somewhere to park the car, and then we'll go in search of swimwear and such,' Matt said.

It didn't suit Zoe, but it was the sensible course and she could raise no feasible objection.

Having dropped off Camille and Tony, complete with his crutches, Matt found a parking space without too much difficulty, beating other fuming motorists because of his knowledge of the area. He then led Zoe directly to a smart boutique that would supply all their needs.

'Do you want a one-piece or a two-piece suit?' he asked.

Having already spotted some of the topless love-lies on the beach, Zoe wondered stupidly

165

if he meant a top piece and a bottom piece or just a bottom piece. If she'd thought about it she would have said a one-piece to make her sunbathing intentions firmly known, because he was obviously not asking if she wanted half a bikini. At least, she didn't think he was! 'A two-piece,' she said firmly, bringing a smile to Matt's lips.

'What color? Black to match your mood, or green to match your jealousy?'

'I am not in a black mood, and what have I got to be jealous about?'

He shrugged, his mocking smile staying resolutely in place. 'I could give you a third choice.'

'And what would that be?'

'Blue to match your eyes.'

'You choose for me.'

'That's an intriguing offer. Dare you abide by my choice?'

Now that she came to think about it, that had been very reckless of her. She had already taken a look round at the selection on display; some were so scanty that they were practically indecent and would hardly cover the essentials. Camille might be happy to expose herself, but Zoe most certainly wasn't. But his eyes were challenging her to back down, and for that reason she wouldn't.

'Of course,' she said, her chin jutting out in defiance.

He went over to a counter, sorted about for

a few moments, then returned with his selection. 'Here you are. Blue to match your eyes. The fitting room is through there. Try it on. If it fits all right and meets with your approval, leave it on.'

To her relief there seemed to be more to this bikini than there was to the ones on display. In the privacy of the fitting room she soon found out that it was a perfect fit. It was the briefest she had ever worn, but what would have been regarded as daring by home standards would seem quite modest here.

She came out smiling, received a bag from the assistant for the purpose of carrying away the garments she had removed, then turned to Matt. 'Thank you,' she said.

He knew exactly what she was thanking him for. 'That's all right. I'll admit, I was tempted to teach you a lesson. But I couldn't go through with it.'

'It was kind of you to spare my blushes. I'm grateful.'

'You've got it all wrong. If just the two of us had been going to a secluded beach I happen to know about I wouldn't have been quite so generous with you. I couldn't go through with it because I would have been jealous as hell of what all the other guys would see.' He filled her arms with beach towels and a bag which she presumed contained suntan lotion. 'Hang on to these for a moment. I found myself in the same predicament as you.' With that he went off to the men's changing rooms, dangling a pair of black swimming trunks in his fingers.

They returned to find that Tony and Camille had hired beach mattresses and were stretched out on theirs. In the garden at Les Charmettes Tony had sunbathed with just his shirt off. His plaster cast looked incongruous with his swimming trunks, even though he had matched the color. Zoe's first glimpse of Camille made her swallow. Both her sundress and the top half of her bikini lay on the edge of her mattress. She was on her stomach, but how long before she flipped over onto her back?

Zoe slid out of her sundress and lay down on her stomach, cradling her head on her folded arms, cautiously shading the nape of her neck with her sunhat. She gasped as a trickle of cold suntan lotion hit her back. She didn't need to open her eyes to know that the hands smoothing it over her belonged to Matt.

The strap of her bikini top must have got in his way. Deftly he unhooked it. 'Don't worry, I'll fasten it again. What I said earlier still goes,' he said softly, so only she could hear.

His fingers worked in a slow circular motion that relaxed her and was pleasant in a drowsily sensual way. His hands moved up to mold the muscles of her shoulders, then down past her shoulder blades, working the lotion well into her waist and down the small of her back to the edge of her bikini briefs.

Despite the quivering of alerted nerve ends and the quickening of her breath, she felt herself slipping deeper into a dreamy kind of languor. The soporific effect melted her bones. There was a pause in the proceedings as he tipped more lotion into his hands. It was transferred to the tops of her arms and the vulnerable area of her thighs. The time he spent was split equally, it was just that one region was rather more electrically aware of the long caressing strokes than the other.

'Turn over and I'll do your front.'

In her mindless stupor she started to obey. She had forgotten, as it seemed that he had, that the fastener between her shoulder blades had been unhooked. As she eased up, half turning to face him, her breasts lifted free from the bikini cups. His slit eyes rested on her for a warm moment, the stirring of his lashes betraying the intensity of his look. She was down again in an instant. He reached over, and a lightning-quick flick of his fingers brought her top securely back into place. It was all accomplished so quickly that neither of the other two could have seen, even if they'd been alert and watching. Tony's and Camille's eyes were closed, however, and they were so still they could have been asleep.

'I can do my front myself,' Zoe croaked, scrambling to sit up, then cupping her hands and holding them out to receive some of the

169

lotion.

'As you like.' Matt moved away and dropped lithely by Camille's side, giving her a nudge that made her lashes flutter up. 'Your turn now.'

Zoe closed her eyes and turned away from Camille's appreciative purrs and ecstatic moans. If the question arose as to which of them did Camille's front, Zoe didn't hear it.

The sun beat down in golden waves. It was beginning to penetrate Zoe's mind that she'd sun-bathed long enough, with her fair skin it would be suicidal not to go in search of some shade, when Matt said, 'Anyone for a swim?'

Tony, who had stirred from his somnolence by this time, said, 'Much as I'd love to, obviously I can't.'

'I'm coming,' Zoe announced. It would get rid of the oily lotion. It wouldn't take long for her bikini to dry, and then she could cover up with her sundress.

'What about you, Camille?'

'No, I don't think so, Matt.'

'That's strange. I've never known you not to join in for a swim. You're usually the first one nattering to go in. Aren't you feeling well?'

'To tell you the truth, I don't feel too good.'

'Perhaps you've been in the sun too long,' Zoe said. Camille had seemed in top form when they came out, but she didn't look at all well now.

Camille sent her a scathing look. 'Don't be

stupid. With my coloring I can stay out in the sun all day without effect. My stomach feels a bit queasy, that's all.'

'It's true,' Tony vouched foster. 'Camille laps the sun up. It must have been something you ate, Camille.'

'Yes, it must have been. Enjoy your swim, you two. Don't bother about me.'

Laughing at Camille's petulance, giving no warning of what he was going to do, Matt turned, scooped Zoe up, and, ignoring her protests, ran into the water with her, not letting her go until it swirled almost to his waist, then throwing her in.

'You beast!' she gasped on coming up, but laughter spilled out of her eyes.

'Come on,' he invited, striking out.

For a short distance she kept alongside him, but his stroke was too powerful for her and she found herself trailing behind, admiring the effortless way he cut through the water.

Tired, exhilarated, she floated on her back, drifting, staring up at the incredibly blue sky. Strong hands pulled her down again. She screamed, loving it, coming up sputtering but laughing. She caught him off balance and then it was her turn to push him under. He retaliated, grabbing her legs and winding them round his waist so that she was riding him. Their eyes were level. For a moment she drowned in the inscrutable depths of his. She was still laughing, but her laugh was shaky.

She wriggled free; the lightness of the mood returned, and when they did run out of the water they were as uninhibited as children.

'That was fantastic,' she said, twisting her hair to wring out the excess water, then patting herself with the beach towel before flinging it down on her mattress and falling on top of it to complete the drying process.

They had a late lunch in a harbor café. Her activities in the water had made Zoe ravenous. She started off with truffle pâté on a crisp green salad bed, then salmon mousse, followed by kidneys in wine, and she finished off with mountain raspberries and whipped cream.

As they came out of the café Matt said, 'I suppose you want to walk that off?'

Zoe looked at Tony, anticipating an objection to being left alone again. He didn't look too pleased, but he said, 'Off you go. I'll find a perch by the harbor and wait for you. You can collect me when you're ready.'

Camille said that she would stay and keep Tony company. She had merely picked at her food, and Zoe guessed that she still didn't feel well and wasn't up to any excess effort.

Matt and Zoe set off to walk through the old town. It was a joy to wander through, and Zoe found it easier to imagine that it had been built up from a poor fishing village to its present lush prosperity than she had on the fashionable beach front.

When she mentioned this Matt nodded in

agreement. 'It's hard to believe St. Tropez hasn't always been the haunt of film stars and tycoons. Before that it was a painters' haven. Originally it was a Greek trading port. But do you know how it got its name?'

'No.'

'Nero executed the Christian Torpetius at Pisa and put the corpse in a boat with a cock and a dog to feed on it. The legend goes that the boat drifted ashore months later, with the body untouched. The fishermen promptly named their collection of huts St. Torpes.'

'That's fascinating,' she said.

They seemed to have reached some unspoken truce. It was therefore all the more surprising when Matt suddenly rounded on her and said, 'When are you going to end this farce of an engagement? The pretense you're keeping up is ridiculous.'

'It's neither ridiculous nor a pretense,' she said, bristling. 'It's a proper engagement.'

'You'll never marry him.'

'I will,' she insisted, stalking on ahead. But whether she meant it as firmly as it sounded, or was merely saying it to protect herself from Matt out of force of habit, she didn't know.

She tried to block out the other alternative that was rising up in her mind: that she was making a big noise to incite Matt's angry reaction. That she wanted him to shout her down on this score. Denying that thought was as hopeless as trying to shut it out. Thoughts like that didn't knock and politely ask if they could come in, they were in before you knew it.

Why was she tearing herself apart? She'd been hurt and humiliated once. Matt had left her without a goodbye. He'd do the same again. She had to be mad. Sun-crazed.

A splintering pain shot across her forehead. Perhaps that was it . . . Perhaps she'd had too much sun after all. The sinking feeling in her stomach wiped out that speculation. It would be nice to think there was a physical reason for the way she felt, but she knew that her condition was emotional and that she would be fooling herself if she believed otherwise.

They made a silent return to pick up the car. Zoe held her tongue on the torment of her thoughts; Matt's face was closed to her, its only animation the cynicism in his eyes. It seemed a million years since they'd cast their differences aside and played happily together, their moods as buoyant as the water they'd ducked each other in.

It was a relief to collect Camille and Tony. Whatever had been ailing Camille was completely gone. Both her health and her spirits had been restored to sparkling form; on the way back it was Camille's bright chatter that shifted the emphasis from the strain that existed between Zoe and Matt and went a long way to lightening the atmosphere.

They stopped for a meal just short of Les

Pins, and this time the roles were reversed. It was Zoe who picked at her food and Camille who made up for her lack of lunch and ate ravenously. Matt dropped Zoe and Tony off at Les Charmettes and then took Camille home.

Even though it was late, Zoe and Tony didn't hurry to bed. Hannah was still up, and they stayed chatting over a nightcap for quite a long while. Zoe couldn't remember what they talked about. Her headache was still banging against her temples, robbing her of concentration. Matt still hadn't returned by the time Zoe did eventually escape to bed.

CHAPTER NINE

Matt left for home the next day. Zoe watched him go with both relief and a strange aching sadness. He went off in his truck with as little ceremony as when he had arrived.

At least this time he hadn't gone without saying goodbye. Did that make it better or worse? There had been nothing in his eyes to suggest that before too long he would be saying hello again.

Camille hadn't gone back with him, as Zoe's inquiry revealed. Apparently André Dupont had persuaded his granddaughter to stay a while longer. But Zoe couldn't help wondering if it wasn't the other way round, that perhaps

175

Camille had failed to persuade Matt to take her back with him.

A few days after Matt's departure an opportunity occurred for Zoe to ask Hannah something which had been bothering her.

'Hannah, while Tony's not around'—he was in his room catching up on his letter writing— 'there's something I'd like to ask you. Please yourself whether you answer me or not. It's none of my business. I've no right to ask, because it's an unpardonable intrusion into your family privacy, but—'

'It can't be that, Zoe, whatever it is. You're going to be part of this family; which makes all the difference. So go ahead and ask. I can always reserve the right to change my mind and not give you an answer if I find that it's *too* sticky.'

'It's about Matt, actually.'

'Is it now?' Hannah said, her gaze floating shrewdly over Zoe's troubled face.

'It's something Tony said about Matt. Naturally, it's his version. I wondered if yours was the same.' Zoe spotted the thoughtful look in Hannah's eyes. If she was reading this right, it came to her that she shouldn't have doubted Tony. In Hannah's estimation, she should, as a loving fiancée, have believed implicitly that what Tony said had to be the truth, without needing confirmation. She wouldn't have questioned anything that Matt had told her. Oh well, having gone that far she had to go on.

'I understand that Matt and Tony's father started out as equal partners, and that Matt bought Tony's father out.'

'Yes, that is so.'

'Tony is under the impression that Matt cheated his father. And so Tony feels cheated. He thinks that he should be Matt's equal partner and not just an employee.'

'Oh, dear. It's very sticky. You're not going to like what I have to say. That is,' Hannah qualified, 'it's not going to put Tony in a favorable light.'

'That can't be helped.'

'No, I don't suppose it can.' Hannah sighed deeply. 'I must tell you a little about Tony's father, my late son-in-law. I don't like speaking ill of the dead, but Edward Talbot was a weak man. Full of charm, of course, with good looks and a silver tongue that could talk the birds out of the trees, so I could understand what Nerissa saw in him, but he was lazy. He wanted all the good things in life, he had very expensive tastes, but he wanted these things without working for them. When he first went into business with Matt it seemed an excellent arrangement. Looking back, Matt must have had some awareness, but he didn't say anything. It only came to light who was putting the real effort in when Matt was out of commission?"

'Out of commission?'

'Matt had an accident while driving a truck.

177

It's said that over half the road accidents to British motorists on the Continent occur within 150 kilometers of leaving the Channel ports, because of tight schedules and unfamiliar driving conditions. But Matt wasn't the one at fault. He never set himself an impossible target, and he was used to driving on the Continent. It was a crazy vacationer who hadn't left himself time to catch his ferry on the homeward trip. He had three children in the car and he was tearing up the road. Matt could have plowed into the car, and being in the much bigger vehicle he stood a chance of getting away comparatively unhurt, or he could have taken a foolhardy risk and swerved to avoid it. If you've come to know Matt at all during your stay here, you won't need me to tell you what action he took.'

'The foolhardy risk?' The only lie she had ever found him out in. I might take the odd calculated risk, he had told her quite recently, but never foolhardy ones. But he had—once.

'He swerved, turned the truck over, and spent the next six months in hospital. The main worry was his right eye.'

'That faint scar across it?'

'Yes. Brilliant surgery was performed on him, then complete rest was ordered. In doing as he was told, and saving his eye, he almost lost his business. Edward let it run completely down. If the boot had been on the other foot Matt would have worked himself into the ground to keep things stable for Edward's return. Edward was simply too lazy to bother. Matt decided that if he was going to work round the clock to get himself out of the red it was going to be for himself and not for someone who wasn't worth it. If cheating Edward Talbot was giving him an ultimatum, accept what's on the table or we'll both sit back and wait for the receiver to come in, then, yes, Matt cheated him. In my book it's the other way round. Because of Edward's initial connection with the business Matt has always felt under an obligation to keep Tony in a secure job. I think Tony is cheating on Matt in not being grateful. He should show a bit of loyalty instead of complaining of injustices done to him. If Tony wants what Matt has got, then he should do what Matt has done, start at the bottom and get it for himself instead of looking for the easy option. Tony is my grandson, my only grandchild, and I love him very much, but I'm not blind to his faults. You asked, and couldn't lie to you. I had to say nothing, which would have been as good as saying that what Tony said about Matt was true, or tell you the facts. I didn't have a choice, did I? I only hope that I haven't lowered Tony too much in your eyes.'

'Strangely enough, you haven't. If anything, it's made me understand him better. Anyone would find it difficult to live up to Matt's example. Tony never had a chance. He could

179

never accomplish what Matt has, even if he lived to be a hundred; he's too much his father's son. He probably realized all that at an early age, so he didn't even try . . . It's all so clear now. Matt's a fine person, and I'm not minimizing what he's done with his life, made of himself, it's just that Tony comes out of a different mold. Matt's like a robot the way he goes after things. In a way, it's a little frightening.'

'You think that Matt's got no tender feelings?'

Was that what she'd implied? 'I don't know.'

'Sometimes what we are isn't entirely in our own hands, as you've just so rightly pointed out. Matt can't help being like he is any more than Tony can. Spare some of your compassion for Matt. Perhaps life has made him that way. His accident robbed him of more than you realize. Brilliant surgery saved his eye, and his own efforts saved his business, but he lost the girl he loved.'

'Yes, I remember you telling me there was a girl in his life. Was she very lovely?'

'I wouldn't know. I never met her. Matt said she was beautiful, but it must have been a superficial beauty. She can't have been very lovely inside. I hated to see Matt so miserable, it tore me apart, and I begged him to get word to her about what had happened, but he said it would be no use. She was only interested in his position and his money. As he was without

180

both at the time he had nothing to offer her that she wanted. He didn't want her to see him as he was. He said it would torture him, although how he could be any more tortured than he was, I failed to see. However, Matt knew this girl, I didn't. I had to trust him to know how she would react.'

'You didn't know her? Not even her . . . her name?'

'I didn't have a name; I didn't know where she lived. I've asked myself since, had I known, would I have overruled Matt and got in touch with her? In my ignorance it was easier to go along with Matt's wish that I didn't. Not that I agreed with him. I like things out in the open, and I told him as much. Recently I've wondered if I was right to let it rest there. I ought to have been more persistent. I might have talked him into letting me contact the girl, have a word with her, get a feeling for the situation for myself. What if Matt was wrong in his estimation of her? That's the question I've found myself asking over and over again just lately. Men, women too for that matter, can be, peculiarly blind to the truth when they're in love!'

Zoe was too busy with her own thoughts to perceive the shrewd way Hannah was looking at her. 'When . . . when did all this happen? How long ago was Matt's accident?'

'Let me see . . . Time goes so quickly when you're getting older, but it must be getting on

181

for . . .' Her brow farrowed in deep concentration. 'Yes, it must be all of five years ago.'

'Thank you for telling me, Hannah.'

She knew that she had piqued Hannah's curiosity, just as hers had been aroused when Hannah first spoke to her about the girl in Matt's past, but it couldn't be helped.

'Thank you,' she repeated, rising abruptly, needing to be alone to think things out.

When Hannah had first mentioned it, why hadn't she probed? In being sensitive to Hannah's feelings, honoring her reluctance to speak of a matter that was private to Matt, she felt that valuable time had been wasted.

Up in her room, she paced the floor restlessly. Five years ago! She was the girl, the girl whom Matt had been certain would turn her back on him in his misfortune. Miss Fortune. That damned name. It had been a bitter joke between them. He had asked her if it would have made any difference to the way she felt about him if he'd had nothing. She had replied truthfully that it would. He had taken it that she just wanted him for his money. He had thought she was like his brother-in-law and his nephew—Nerissa, too, for that matter—out for what she could get. The picture that Zoe had now was that even if they had bled him white, they still wouldn't have been satisfied. Edward Talbot was dead, of course, so that only left Nerissa and Tony to be

182

bitter and vindictive, jealous of Matt instead of being glad for him and proud to be associated with him. They wanted the high life but didn't want to make the effort of earning it. They wanted it to be provided for them, and Matt thought she was the same. Her glib reply that he wouldn't have had the same fascination for her if he hadn't been so successful had convinced him that he was right. With relatives like his, no wonder he was suspicious and took the jaundiced viewpoint. She had meant that he wouldn't have been the same Matt without his ambition and intelligence and commanding personality. It was the things that would get him to the top and keep him there that had attracted her, not the rewards!

But he hadn't understood. Oh, Matt, those wretched years . . . The thought of him lying hurt in hospital and her not being there with him tore at her heart. She cried for the hopelessness of it all.

She dried her eyes. It wasn't hopeless at all. She had to end her engagement to Tony. Her feelings for him had never been strong enough. He hadn't been able to stamp Matt out of her heart. There wasn't a man alive who could do that. And then she had to go back home and seek Matt out. And they had to talk. Perhaps nothing would come of it, but they had to talk.

Camille and her grandfather, André Dupont, were coming to dinner. The tangle of her own personal life would have to be put away for the time being. She had to get ready, then put on a bright smile, and do nothing to cast a shadow on the evening's festivities.

She used extra makeup to counteract the natural sparkle that was missing and managed to get back downstairs minutes prior to the arrival of the guests. Hannah liked the courtesy of everyone being there for the greeting.

Camille was looking especially beautiful. There was something about her, a glow that didn't come from makeup but was born from within. Yet at the same time there was something about her that undermined that look of well-being. She had forsaken her favorite red and wore a dress of sharp citrus yellow which showed off her luscious curves to perfection.

Zoe turned her eyes to Camille's grandfather. Rich, distinguished, and handsome, André Dupont doted on Camille and would obviously tear the earth apart to grant her smallest whim. Some would say 'lucky Camille,' but Zoe wasn't so sure. The most precious things in life had to be given freely. They become valueless when bought for hard cash.

Would Hannah and Monsieur Dupont ever make a match? she wondered. She had known Hannah for a short time, yet she felt deeply a part of her life. It was odd to think that in ending her engagement to Tony, if things didn't work out between her and Matt, she would become nothing to Hannah and might never see her again. It was an unhappy, chilling thought. She dared not pin her hopes on making a future with Matt. In explaining what had happened five years ago, Hannah had said he'd lost the girl he loved. But had Matt said that in so many words, or had Hannah romanticized Matt's feelings and made that assumption herself? Matt had never told her that he loved her. He wanted her in a physical way, he had never made any bones about that, but love was another matter entirely.

'What a very deep look.'

Zoe turned to André Dupont, who had made the remark, and was sitting next to her at the table. 'I'm sorry, Monsieur. I was miles away.'

'Really? I should have thought only inches,' he said, referring to the fact that Tony was sitting on her other side. 'Being in love is not the simple state the popular ballads lead us to believe. It can be a complex and traumatic business.'

It was an observation that followed her own life too closely and invited Zoe's sharp intake of breath, but then it occurred to her that Monsieur Dupont was talking to her in an abstract fashion and that his eyes were on his granddaughter.

185

His concentration directed her own gaze there. She saw the smile die on Camille's lips and noticed the glazed look in the girl's eyes before her lashes fluttered down, and then Camille folded like a rag doll and with boneless grace slid to the floor.

Zoe had never seen anyone faint so beautifully. At first no one seemed to realize what had happened, and then everyone moved of one accord. Tony was hampered by his crutches, but between them Zoe and André Dupont managed to transfer Camille to the sofa. She came round almost immediately, looking bewildered and obviously wondering what all the commotion was about.

'You fainted,' Hannah explained gently.

'What a silly thing to do!' Camille still looked confused, despite the laugh that came to her lips.

'Perhaps I should take you home,' André Dupont said with some perplexity, not seeming to know what would be best.

'But, grandpapa, why? I'm all right now,' Camille protested.

'I've never known you to faint before,' he said, his eyes appealing to Hannah for guidance.

'There's a first time for everything,' Camille replied nonchalantly. 'Honestly, grandpapa, I feel wonderful, so don't fuss.'

'Young girls do have these peculiar turns, André. I wouldn't attach too much importance

186

to the matter, if I were you,' Hannah comforted.

André's gaze rested on Camille, who now seemed quite recovered; her color was back to normal, and she was preening herself in a manner that suggested she was enjoying the attention. His anxiety lifted. 'Yes, I suppose you are right. It would be a pity to curtail such a very pleasant evening.'

'Good.' Hannah's tone was brisk. 'Let's return to the table.'

The incident was forgotten and not referred to again until the guests' departure.

After depositing goodbye kisses on both of Hannah's cheeks, Camille said, 'Thank you for a perfect meal and a lovely time.' Then she added apologetically, 'I'm sorry to have caused that little stir during dinner.'

'You must not give it another thought, *mon enfant.* These things happen. You might telephone me tomorrow to set my mind at rest that all is well with you.'

'I'll do better than that. I'll come round, if I may, and then you can see for yourself.'

'You are always welcome here, you know that.'

As André Dupont took his leave of her, Hannah said, her voice as light as a summer breeze, 'Just as a precaution, why not let Camille be seen by her doctor?'

'I am sure it is nothing, but perhaps that is not such a bad idea.' There was no alarm in the dark eyes that dipped over the hand. Hannah offered for his parting kiss.

*   *   *

Why it came as a surprise, Zoe would never know. All the clues were there, and yet, as Hannah replaced the telephone receiver the next day, Zoe had no idea of what was coming.

'That was André,' Hannah explained. 'The doctor has just examined Camille. It seems, after all, that André will get his long desired liaison with our family, if not in quite the way he had wished. I don't know how to tell you this, Zoe. I'm very, very sorry, my dear. But Camille is pregnant.'

Camille pregnant. Liaison between the two families. Just who, exactly, was Hannah saying the father was?

'I must telephone Matt,' Hannah said, turning back to the telephone, lifting the receiver, dialing. 'He'll get here on the first available flight.'

CHAPTER TEN

Camille having Matt's child? But Camille was only nineteen, Zoe told herself. Still, what did that have to do with it? Anyway, Zoe had only been nineteen when it had almost happened between them. She wished it had. She wished fiercely that they had made love and a child had resulted . . . Matt's child. She felt sick and miserable and jealous of the new life stirring in Camille. If anyone was to have Matt's baby, it should have been she.

'I'm even sorrier than I thought,' she heard Hannah say as though from a long way away. 'I honestly didn't think you cared all that much.'

'Not care?' She faced Hannah, eyes blazing. 'I love him. I've never loved anyone else, and I never will, as long as I live.'

'Oh, my dear. If I'm surprised, it's because you haven't shown it. Sometimes you've appeared quite cool toward him.'

'It's had to be that way,' Zoe said wearily.

'Tony won't be able to marry you now, you do realize that, of course. The right thing must be done.'

She would do the right thing. She couldn't admit to loving another man and go ahead and marry Tony. 'I'll release him from our engagement, of course.'

'The marriage will have to be arranged as quickly as possible, and quietly. But not too quietly, because that would defeat the object by arousing gossip. Camille has no sisters of her own to take precedence. I don't know how you feel about this, but on the phone André hinted that it might be a kindness on your part to be Camille's chief bridesmaid. It would go a long way to stop the tongues wagging.'

'No, Hannah. I couldn't! That's asking too much of me.'

'Perhaps when you've thought about it . . . Hannah entreated.

'No!' Bitter tears filled Zoe's eyes. 'Why should I? I can't forgive what Matt and Tony have done to me. Between them they've just about destroyed me. Neither of them really cared about me. They used me to settle a difference.'

'I'm deeply disappointed in you, Zoe,' Hannah chided frostily. 'Which is something I never thought I'd hear myself say to you. That remark is beneath your intelligence and an insult to my son. It might be true of Tony, but not of Matt. Matt does not use people.'

'You're right, Hannah. That was unworthy of me and I take it back. Matt doesn't use people.'

'I knew some drama was being played out among the three of you, but I couldn't make a lot of sense of it. Still can't, for that matter. You and Matt seemed to know one another too well to have met only recently through Tony. I kept getting strong signals that you'd known each other before. You could even be the girl he lost five years ago. You are, aren't you?'

'Yes. I wouldn't have thrown him over because he couldn't give me the good times. I would have stuck by him, no matter what. I thought he'd walked out on me. I didn't know he'd been involved in an accident until you told me. You've got to believe that.'

'I do believe it.' A small sigh escaped Hannah's lips. 'It's Matt you should be telling, not me. Although if you meant what you said earlier, and much as I would like to I can't doubt your sincerity, I don't suppose there would be much point. I must be losing my grip, because I could have sworn that you and . . . well, never mind.'

What was the matter with Hannah? Wasn't she thinking straight? Of course there would be no point now.

The other thing Hannah had said was right about Matt not using people. When he had taken her in his arms it had been because he wanted to and not to score off Tony. But he had also made love to Camille, and Camille was carrying his child and so he had an obligation to marry her. She could understand any man finding Camille irresistible, she was luscious and inviting, but why hadn't Matt resisted?

Zoe had known from the beginning that Camille had lost her innocence, and she was pretty certain that Matt hadn't been the one to take it away from her in the first place. When she was nineteen, he had known by instinct that she had never been with a man, and some rigid moral code had stopped him at the last moment. Oh, Matt, why? The odd thing was, she didn't know if she was asking herself why

191

Matt hadn't made love to her then or why he'd had to go with Camille now.

A glass of water was placed in her hand. Hannah gently coaxed, 'Here, drink this, although really I think it should be brandy. You've gone as white as a sheet. I shouldn't have spoken so sharply to you just now. I didn't make allowances for your suffering.'

On taking a sip, Zoe said, 'Please don't be too nice to me, Hannah, you'll make me cry. I don't want to go soggy-eyed to Tony to return his ring, and that's something I must do straight away.'

'Yes, dear. I'm sorry, sorry for all of us, that things haven't worked out the way you wanted. I'm even sorrier still that they haven't worked out the way I would have liked,' Hannah added ambiguously.

'Thank you, Hannah.' What else could she say. 'I'll go find Tony.'

But first she went up to her room for the box the ring had come in from the jeweler's shop. She put the ring in the box, then placed the box in an envelope on which she wrote: *I'm sorry it had to be like this, Tony. The contents will explain it all. No words necessary.* Then she went downstairs to find him.

He was where he usually was, in the garden. She handed him the bulky envelope. He accepted it, read what she'd written on the front, and tore it open. Shrugging, he put the ring box in his pocket.

192

'Good old never-make-a-fuss Zoe!' he scoffed, a look of bravado coming to his face. 'It never ceases to amaze me the calm way you take things. I expected fireworks and recriminations.'

That's what Zoe had expected from him. 'What for, Tony?' she asked carefully.

'For giving you such a rotten deal, of course. I'm sorry. God, how inadequate that sounds, but it's true. I'm sorry for you, and selfish to the end, I'm just a little bit sorry for myself. Quite recently Nan remarked that I was a better person for knowing you, and I think she's right. If we'd stuck together you might have reformed me totally. As it is, well, Camille and I are out of the same mold. And you could say that I've landed on my feet. André Dupont is comfortably off. Camille is his only grandchild and will inherit the lot. On reflection, my position is really quite enviable.' Suddenly he dropped the light, jocular tone to ask, 'So why don't I feel better about things?'

Zoe hardly dared to believe the implication of Tony's words. Was he saying that he was the father of Camille's child, not Matt? All she could feel was stunned incredulity.

'I don't know,' she said, her words reflecting her perplexity: 'You tell me why you don't feel better about things.'

'Because I think I was falling in love with you.'

'Weren't you in love with me when you

193

asked me to marry you? The truth, Tony. You owe me that.'

'Yes, I guess I do. And so, no I wasn't in love with you. I was attracted to you, and I want you to know that my affection for you has steadily grown, but my main reason was wanting to triumph over Matt.'

'But you weren't aware that I knew Matt. Or were you?'

'Yes, I knew. Have you found out yet why Matt didn't come back to you five years ago?'

'Yes. Hannah told me about his accident.' She gasped. 'You knew! You knew there was a girl in his life. You've known all this time that I was that girl. And you let me go on thinking that he didn't return because he didn't want me, even though you and I had talked about it.'

'Don't look at me like that, Zoe. I didn't have to tell you now, and I'm only doing so to try to make amends. I knew all about the message you got to the effect that Matt wasn't available when you phoned to ask about him. That message came via me. I visited Matt in hospital and he told me to instruct the staff to say what they did should you inquire.'

'Matt thought he had nothing to offer me, and he didn't want my pity,' she said in a low voice.

'Something like that. I thought he was being stupid; it was obvious that he was eating his heart out for you. I couldn't understand his reasoning.'

Her lashes flew up. 'And when we met, and you heard my name, you knew who I was!' The accusation scraped rawly on her throat. She seemed to be fighting back both tears and laughter.

'Yes . . . Said cold, it sounds horrible, and I'm ashamed. At the beginning I didn't see you for yourself. You had something I found attractive, and that was Matt's interest. He's always scored in life. It would have been something to put one over on him. To get my hands on something he wanted appealed to me very much.'

'How did you know that Matt still wanted me after all that time?'

'When he got the business on its feet again he set someone on trying to find you. But you'd moved and changed jobs and couldn't be traced. I couldn't believe my luck when I met you—not strictly by chance, incidentally. I fixed the first meeting. I overheard your name in conversation. It had to be you. I knew the personal details about you from the inquiries Matt had been making your age, coloring. There couldn't be two redheads in that age group with such an unusual name. And so I made a fast play for you. I wanted to keep you secret from Matt until after the nuptial knot was firmly tied—that would really have rubbed his nose in it—but it didn't come off. He made one of his famous unscheduled visits before the wedding, and your identity couldn't be withheld any longer. You've got to hand it to Matt, though, he was a cunning old dog, setting me up like that.'

'You mean by taking you out and getting you drunk?'

'That wasn't all he did. The party he arranged for me wasn't the traditional stag thing. Camille was among the people he invited. He laid it on the mat for me. I've always fancied Camille, I won't deny that, but she's never looked at me before. It's always been Matt. She was all over him that night, but he wasn't playing, so she turned to someone who would play—me! It started off for laughs. I took her home and we started messing around, just kissing. We'd both had too much to drink. Before I realized what was happening, we were in bed together. Camille had dug out a bottle of Scotch and we'd started drinking again, and so it's all pretty hazy in my mind. But I know we made love. I woke up with an awful hangover, which was how I came to fall down the steps and break my stupid leg on leaving Camille's apartment.'

'That was a lucky break for both of us. It would have been a disaster if our wedding had taken place as planned.' It didn't bear thinking of. 'What you said just now about beginning to fall in love with me . . . well, that wasn't true. You were just considering my feelings. You can't feel that way about me because you're in

196

love with Camille. I can't believe my own stupidity. I've seen the way you look at her. Why it didn't occur to me, I don't know. I guess I've been too wrapped up in my own affairs. I'm pleased for you, Tony. It's not the best way to start a marriage, so it's up to you to make it a good one. I hope that you and Camille will be very happy.'

'Thank you, Zoe. That's sweet of you.'

'One thing puzzles me. I thought the steps you fell down were at the club you'd been to. What was it called—the Ace of Clubs?'

'There are no steps at the Ace of Clubs,' he said sheepishly.

'I see. The girl who phoned to say you'd been taken to hospital. That was Camille? Your mother said she spoke with a foreign accent. That's really ironic! Your mother said she thought the girl was French because her voice was like Camille's. No wonder. It *was* Camille!'

'Yes. And that's it. Now you know it all. The whole sordid story.'

'Thank you for telling me, Tony.' She ought to be furious with him. But she was so unbelievably happy that it was Tony, not Matt, who was responsible for Camille's condition that she couldn't get her anger anywhere near the boil. She couldn't stop smiling.

'Thinking about it, did I have much option?'

'No. So perhaps I mean for the way you've told me, fairly and truthfully. It's made me

197

hope there's still a chance for Matt and me to find happiness together. Your grandmother phoned Matt straight away, asking him to come. Because Matt was head of the family, and because of the longstanding friendship between the two families, Hannah had felt that Matt should pay André Dupont the courtesy of talking to him, conferring with him about the arrangements for the wedding, and possibly allaying any fears about Tony's willingness to shoulder his responsibilities. It had not been for the reason she had thought, Zoe realized, hugging herself for joy. 'I was all set to pack up and get a plane out before he arrived, which would have created even more misunderstanding between us. So I owe you a big thank you.'

'Don't pin any halos on me, Zoe. I know that Nan's phoned Matt to come. She buttonholed me before you did.'

'Just now, while I was upstairs?'

'I suppose so.'

'That wasn't the first you knew of the baby, was it?'

'It was the first time I got it officially, but Camille suspected she might be pregnant the day we went to St. Tropez, remember?'

'Ah, yes, her indisposition wasn't because of something she ate!' Zoe observed wryly.

'Anyway, to get back to what Matt's reaction will be. To say he isn't going to be pleased is the understatement of the year. Camille isn't some girl I've picked up off the street; we've known her since we were kids. It's to my advantage to make my peace with you. You have a lot of influence with Matt, and I want you on my side.'

'Perhaps that's the way it is, and perhaps not. I think you're so happy yourself with what has happened that some deep down generous streak, which you're fighting to deny, wants me to be happy, too. So, again, thank you, Tony.' She kissed him lightly on the cheek and walked on air as she left him to find Hannah again.

'I've changed my mind, Hannah,' she said without ceremony. 'If Camille wants me, I'd love to be bridesmaid for her.'

'What brought that about?'

'I jumped to a silly conclusion. You'll never believe who I thought the father of Camille's child was.'

'You mean you didn't think Tony was responsible?'

'No. I thought it was Matt.'

'But how absurd! Admittedly, I'm surprised by all this. I knew that Tony had a weakness for Camille, but it seemed hopeless, because Camille's always had an outsize crush on Matt. But she's a child in his eyes. He was always very protective of her; he might not have put her in her place too severely to avoid hurting her feelings, but he never intentionally led her on. I don't know why Camille turned to Tony—perhaps out of pique—but that's just a

199

wild guess.' For a wild guess, it was pretty accurate, Zoe thought. 'It seemed that I was going to lose you, Zoe. Is there a possibility that that may not be so?'

'I don't know.'

'When I spoke to Matt on the phone, he said he'd pull strings and be here as soon as possible. He asked how you had taken the news. I said you were utterly miserable and that you'd taken it very badly indeed. When he gets here—this evening, I hope—I think he's going to have a pleasant surprise.'

*   *   *

Tony and Hannah had accepted an invitation to dine with Camille and her grandfather. Zoe had been included in the invitation, but she had declined. If Matt got there that night, she wanted to be waiting for him.

She dressed with care, choosing the white dress she'd worn when Matt had arrived the last time and found her in the garden. She brushed her hair until it was like silken fire and was extra generous with her favorite perfume. She fastened Matt's pendant round her neck. Her fingers were shaking in anticipation of his coming. What if they were all wrong? She had never heard it from Matt's lips that there was a valid reason for his nonreturn five years ago. What if he'd dropped her because she had ceased to interest him? In what way did she interest him now? Did he only want a beautiful but brief affair, or did he have it in mind to spend the rest of his life with her?

She put off eating, although she hadn't been able to eat any lunch and had promised Hannah faithfully that she would have something when they left. She was too choked up, frightened, and excited to eat. And in any case, she wanted to wait and eat with Matt. She felt as though she didn't even want to breathe without Matt.

She heard the car pull into the drive. She had the door open and was outside in time to see him pay the taxi driver off. She wanted to run to him, but she couldn't. His face was visible in the light cast from the house. It was so grave and solemn. He looked as if he'd thrown himself together, pulling on the first clothes that had come to hand in order to catch his plane. He wasn't even carrying a suitcase she noticed as he came striding toward her. His arms went round her and he bundled her inside.

'It's going to be all right, Zoe. He wasn't right for you.'

'I know.'

'You're well rid of him.'

'I know.'

'He didn't love you in the way you should be loved. He was attracted to you for all the wrong . . . What did you say?'

201

'I said I know that Tony wasn't right for me and that it's better that he's out of my life, and I'm fully aware that he wanted me for all the wrong reasons. I can't begin to explain what a tremendous relief I feel.'

'But on the phone . . . mother said you were inconsolable, desolate beyond belief. She said she'd never in all her life seen anyone crack up the way you did.'

'That was when I thought it was you and Camille.'

'Me? But Camille's only a child.'

'If you think that, you haven't been looking at her properly lately.'

'That's probably true. I haven't been looking at anyone properly lately. All I've been able to see is you. You've superimposed yourself so firmly on my mind that there's been no room for anyone or anything else. You've put me through every kind of mental and physical torture possible.'

'Oh, Matt, I didn't know.'

'Didn't know! You didn't know what you were doing to me? Now I've heard it all.'

'I thought it was just physical. A need any woman could fill.'

'No, Zoe. I won't say that you're the only woman who has ever filled my arms . . .'

'I wouldn't believe you if you did.'

'. . . but you're the only woman who has ever filled my heart. When I heard that you were the one Tony was going to marry I almost went out of my mind. I tried to kid myself that in the years we'd been apart I'd immortalized what we had, built it up and romanticized it into something larger than life. The value of something lost is invariably magnified out of all proportion, and I thought it might be the same with you. Instead—well, I came round to see you, and instead of making things better, it was a million times worse. I knew I couldn't let Tony have you. I was half crazed wondering what to do.'

'You soon figured something out.'

'It wasn't as calculated as that. Nothing was planned, although all sorts of vague notions were stirring through my mind, such as getting Tony so drunk that he wouldn't be in a fit state for his own wedding. Things just seemed to happen of their own accord. Poor Camille, in a way I feel partly to blame, but I wasn't to know how far things would go. I can't be responsible for that. She was making a tremendous nuisance of herself with me. She's a nice child, but sometimes she can be overpowering, and frankly, I wasn't in the mood for fun and games. She got the message and began to make eyes at Tony.'

'To make you jealous?'

'I was jealous of Tony, all right, as jealous as hell. But not over her, over you. Tony was like a greedy little boy. He'd already got the pick of the crop, but he couldn't resist taking a bite of another cherry when it was dangled under his nose.'

'Tony thinks he's got the pick of the crop with Camille.'

'He's only a boy. What does he know?'

She laughed. It was a lilting, joyous sound. 'What would you have done if Tony hadn't fallen down the stairs and broken his leg on leaving Camille's apartment?'

'You figured it out that he didn't fall down any stairs at the Ace of Clubs?'

'I got it from Tony that there aren't any stairs at the Ace of Clubs. You could have told me that, instead of covering up for him. You covered for him about something else as well.'

'Did I?'

'Don't come the innocent. You were aware from the beginning that Tony knew about us. You knew how guilty I felt about not telling Tony and yet you said nothing.'

'M'm. Found out about that as well, did you?'

'Tony admitted that you passed the message via him that you weren't available if I phoned to inquire. That was horrible. How could you have been cruel enough to instruct anyone to say that to me?'

'I had always stood tall in your eyes. I couldn't bear the thought of your seeing me on my back. I've always thought of myself as being one brave guy. They say everyone is allowed one lapse, and that was mine, my act of cowardice. I was too much of a coward to risk your rejection.'

'So you rejected me.'

'And regretted it a million times. You asked me why I covered for Tony. For various reasons, I suppose, all hinging on the fact that I didn't know how badly you'd got it for him. I didn't want to hurt you by telling you what a scheming louse he was and that he only wanted you—'

'You can say it. He only wanted me to make you squirm.'

'It's better that you said it for me. Secondly, I've never ratted on anyone in my life, and even if I had told you, would you have believed me? Thirdly, I fully intended to take you from him, but in a fair fight. And it's been that, Zoe,' he said, contesting the look she gave him, even if his smile was mischievous. 'While some things are definitely not on, taletelling for example, a little honest to goodness chicanery is not only acceptable but considered fair play.'

'You have a convenient sense of logic.'

'Comes in handy. I don't know what I would have done if Tony hadn't helped me out by breaking a leg, but I would have thought of something to prevent the marriage taking place. There's only one man you're going to marry, and that's me.'

'Am I?'

'You wouldn't be challenging that, would you?'

'No way. Just confirming that I heard you right. I love you, Matt. Love you so much.'

'I love you, Zoe. More than life itself. It's nice that you're willing, it makes it more peaceable, but I had every intention of getting you to the altar even if I had to drag you there by your beautiful hair.' He wound his fingers into it. 'I need a shave. I didn't have time to get one before setting off. Come up with me while I get one now.'

'If I go to your room with you, I don't think I'll get out again before morning.'

His hand left her hair and traced the narrow shoulder strap of her dress. 'That's the general idea.'

She swallowed rawly. They had been so long denied. 'No. Hannah and Tony will be home soon. You know she'll want to see you before going to bed. I'm not starting off on the wrong foot with my future mother-in-law. Is Hannah going to be surprised!' she exclaimed in nervous jubilation.

'I doubt it. Overjoyed, not surprised,' Matt corrected. And she knew that he was right. 'If you won't come with me, I'm not leaving you. Someone might spirit you away.' Gathering her into his arms, he rubbed his bristly chin across her forehead. 'You'll just have to take the rough with the smooth.'

'That's all I ever wanted, Matt. To share the rough with you, as well as the smooth. Instead of sending that snubbing message to be passed on to me, you should have got word to me about your accident.' She lifted her hand; her fingertips delicately followed the faint scar that crossed his eye. 'Oh, my darling, I would have been by your side in a flash, and I never would have left you, no matter what.'

He acknowledged soberly, 'That was a grave mistake on my part. Let's write it off, Zoe, and concentrate on—'

'The future?'

'The immediate present was what I had in mind,' he said, drawing her tenderly closer. 'I've dreamed of this moment, had nightmares that it would never happen.' His lips skimmed over her eyelids, then locked on her mouth.

*   *   *

Matt gave her the choice of going anywhere in the world for their honeymoon, but he hadn't laughed when she expressed a wish to spend the first part of it at the *logis* where they had found shelter from the rain.

Berthe and Jean-Claude Poussin were delighted by the compliment paid to their modest establishment and gave the honeymooners a rapturous welcome. For their wedding night dinner they sat at the same table as before, side by side, barely noticing the celebration meal Jean-Claude had prepared for them. Everything still had the unreality of a dream come true.

'How can I be so lucky?' Matt asked.

'I don't know. I was just asking myself the same thing.'

Madame's eyes followed them with smiling indulgence, and a little nostalgia maybe, as they left the dining room.

Zoe had thought she might be shy, but it seemed the most natural thing in the world to be undressed by Matt. It was a slow and sensuous process with many pauses for the removal of his clothes, in which she assisted, and for an exchange of caresses. When her gentle curves were fully exposed he carried her to the bed. He covered her face with kisses, tasting—the soft texture of her skin, the delicate skin of her eyelids and cheeks, the rich curve of her lips. His hands were so very, very loving, gentle, yet with a magical precision that arrested her breath and made her feel incredibly beloved and cared for. His finger-tips were as expressive of his love as the words he whispered into her ear. Only when all the pleasures possible had been sated, and the expectation of what was to come had been savored to the limits of their joint restraint, did he draw her closer . . . and inexorably closer.

At first it was a gentle slide into ecstasy, a cherishing warmth and an endless sweetness, searing, tender, lifting her and whirling her forward. She was a sapling torn up by a storm and hurled into a new dimension of feeling . . . Sensations she would not have believed possible were gaining on the rapid beat of her heart, overtaking her breath. She could no longer even gasp out his name. Nothing, none of the previous delights, had prepared her for the ultimate joy, this incredulous escalation into the heart of passion's flame, a fire that consumed her, then cradled her in the most sublime peace and contentment she had ever known. Long afterward their bodies and arms were still entwined.

Sleep was a million light years away. Zoe slipped out of bed and crept to the window. Her elbows on the sill, still feeling wrapped in that enchanted bliss, she looked up at the huge moon, a symbol of constancy. The ardent assurance of Matt's love had melted all past anxieties away. Even feeling as smug as she did, she couldn't prevent tears of awe from glistening on her lashes, dazzling diamonds that splintered the moon into a brilliant orb, giving it a new face, and her thoughts a new slant.

Her vision had been splintered in evaluating her own feelings; she hadn't seen the truth of love clearly. Love wasn't any one thing; love was all things. She had been right in thinking that love was constancy, warmth, and caring— that blend of affection was vital—but she had been wrong in not realizing that love was also a burning passion that sometimes felt too hot to handle, that it had a meteoric brightness touched with a little moon madness and a lot of earthly magic.

'Stop that moon gazing and come back to bed,' Matt called out softly. 'You should be asleep.'

'I can sleep later,' she said, anguished at the thought of sleeping away so much happiness.

'Come back to bed,' he instructed thickly. 'We'll both sleep later.'

We hope you have enjoyed this Large Print book. Other Chivers Press or Thorndike Press Large Print books are available at your library or directly from the publishers.

For more information about current and forthcoming titles, please call or write, without obligation, to:

Chivers Large Print
published by BBC Audiobooks Ltd
St James House, The Square
Lower Bristol Road
Bath BA2 3BH
UK
email: bbcaudiobooks@bbc.co.uk
www.bbcaudiobooks.co.uk

OR

Thorndike Press
295 Kennedy Memorial Drive
Waterville
Maine 04901
USA
www.gale.com/thorndike
www.gale.com/wheeler

All our Large Print titles are designed for easy reading, and all our books are made to last.